Christmas really was magic.

Imogen had seen it in her training when she'd worked a shift on the children's ward—seen how, no matter how dire, everyone pulled together and made the impossible work on that day. She had seen it in her own family a few short years ago, and she was seeing it now with his.

Angus, with only an hour's sleep to his name, was trying to work out what parcel Santa had left for whom—because he'd been sure when he'd wrapped them that he'd remember! He was smiling and holding it together, and just doing his very best for the two little people who mattered most.

Imogen was blinking at her rather big pile of presents. A big pile she truly hadn't been expecting.

'From me,' Angus said gruffly, as she pulled back the wrapper on a vast silk bedspread. 'I figured if I can't be with you…'

And it was so nice…too nice. And a whole world away from the time when she'd have to cuddle up to this instead of him.

Imogen crumpled. And she truly didn't know if she was crying because she'd miss him, or crying because right now she missed her little boy, or crying because the one time in her life she had the *crème de la crème* of *everything* lined up and at her service, raring to go, she was in absolutely no position to take what was on offer.

Carol Marinelli recently filled in a form where she was asked for her job title, and was thrilled, after all these years, to be able to put down her answer as 'writer'. Then it asked what Carol did for relaxation, and after chewing her pen for a moment Carol put down the truth—'writing'. The third question asked—'What are your hobbies?' Well, not wanting to look obsessed or, worse still, boring, she crossed the fingers on her free hand and answered 'swimming and tennis'. But—given that the chlorine in the pool does terrible things to her highlights, and the closest she's got to a tennis racket in the last couple of years is watching the Australian Open—I'm sure you can guess the real answer!

Recent titles by the same author:

Medical™ Romance
A DOCTOR, A NURSE: A LITTLE MIRACLE
BILLIONAIRE PRINCE, ORDINARY NURSE*
THE SINGLE DAD'S MARRIAGE WISH

Modern™ Romance
HIRED: THE ITALIAN'S CONVENIENT MISTRESS
ITALIAN BOSS, RUTHLESS REVENGE
EXPECTING HIS LOVE-CHILD*

The House of Kolovsky

ONE MAGICAL CHRISTMAS

BY
CAROL MARINELLI

MILLS & BOON™

Pure reading pleasure™

All the characters in this book have no existence outside the imagination of the author, and have no relation whatsoever to anyone bearing the same name or names. They are not even distantly inspired by any individual known or unknown to the author, and all the incidents are pure invention.

First published in Great Britain 2008
Harlequin Mills & Boon Limited,
Eton House, 18-24 Paradise Road, Richmond, Surrey TW9 1SR

© Carol Marinelli 2008

ISBN: 978 0 263 20380 6

Set in Times Roman 10½ on 12¾ pt
07-1008-43417

Printed and bound in Great Britain
by Antony Rowe Ltd, Chippenham, Wiltshire

ONE MAGICAL CHRISTMAS

For Bob and Glynn
Love you lots
xxx

CHAPTER ONE

'HI THERE! I'm Imogen.'

Accident and Emergency Consultant Angus Maitlin looked up from orders he was hastily writing as, wearing a smile and not a trace of unease, the woman walked towards him.

'Sorry?' Handing his orders to his intern, Angus frowned at the unfamiliar face.

'Heather said I should come introduce myself to you,' she patiently explained, and Angus picked out an Australian accent. 'I've been sent down from Maternity to help with the emergency you're expecting in…'

She watched him glance at her ID badge.

'You're a midwife?'

'And an RN.' Imogen added, without elaborating. Something told her that this good-looking package of testosterone really wasn't in the mood to listen!

'Have you worked here before?' His hands gestured to the frantic Resuscitation area. The five beds were full and one was being cleared for a burn victim trapped in a car on a busy London motorway. 'Do you know the layout?'

'Not yet,' she said, looking around her. 'I've only been in the country two days. Still, I'm sure—'

She didn't have a chance to finish so she just stood there as he stalked off, no doubt to complain to the nursing unit manager. Well, let him complain, Imogen thought—she didn't want to be here and he clearly didn't want her here either! With a bit of luck she'd be sent back to Maternity.

'Heather!' Angus barked, not yet out of Imogen's earshot. 'When I said that I urgently needed more help in Resus I didn't mean you to send in a midwife!'

Angus rarely lost his temper but he was close to it now. The department was full, Resus was full, and his request for more staff had been met by this rather large, grinning woman in a white agency nurse's uniform who had only just set foot in the country!

'I'll come and help if need be,' Heather responded calmly. 'But the nursing co-ordinator did tell me that not only is Imogen a midwife, she's also advanced emergency and ICU trained. Though,' she added sweetly, 'I do have a grad nurse in the observation ward. I can swap her over if you think that would be more—'

'I'll manage,' Angus cut it in curtly, and then changed his mind, closing his eyes for a second and running a hand through his dark blond hair. 'I'm sorry, Heather—I didn't think to ask about her qualifications. It's just when she said that she'd only just arrived here…'

He glanced over to where Imogen stood where he'd rudely left her, and gave a small wince of apology. He expected to receive a rather pained, martyred look back—it would have been what he deserved—only, clearly amused, she merely shrugged and smiled. The strangest thing of all was, given the morning he was having, Angus actually found himself smiling back.

'I'm sure people suffer from burns in Australia!' Heather's sarcasm soon wiped it from his face, though.

'I get it, OK?' He reached for his water bottle at the nurses' station and took a long drink. The patient they were expecting was still being extricated from the car and there was plenty he could be doing in that time, but from the brief description of the horrific injuries that would soon present, Angus guessed a minute to centre himself was probably going to be time well spent.

'Is everything OK, Angus?' Heather Barker also had plenty she could be getting on with but, used to priorities shifting quickly in this busy London accident and emergency department, she took a moment to deal with the latest category one to present. Angus Maitlin, the usually completely together consultant, the utter lynchpin of the department, seemed for once to not be faring so well.

Not that he said it.

Not that he ever said it.

Impossibly busy, he was usually infinitely calm and dependable. Not only did Angus help run the accident and emergency department, he was also married to a successful model, a proud father to two young children *and* had, in the past few years, become something of a TV celebrity. Angus had been asked, by the local television station, to give his medical opinion on post-traumatic stress syndrome. His deep, serious voice, his undeniable good looks, combined with just the right dash of humour, had proved an instant hit, and the cameras, along with the audience, had adored him. Which meant he had been asked back again, and now Angus Maitlin was regularly called on to deliver his particular brand of medicine on a current affairs show. Yet somehow his celebrity status hadn't changed him a jot—Angus still had his priorities well in place—his family first, the emergency department a very close second, or, when the situation demanded, Emergency first, family second, and then, somehow, everything else got slotted in.

Just not today.

Not for the past couple of months, actually.

'Angus?' When he ignored her question Heather rephrased it. 'Is there a problem?'

'Of course not.'

'Anything that you might want to talk about?'

'I'm fine.'

Sitting on a stool, muscular, yet long limbed and elegant, his thick fringe flopping over jade eyes, his immaculately cut suit straining just a touch to contain wide shoulders as he drank some water, Angus Maitlin looked better than fine—the absolute picture of relaxed health, in fact—only everyone in the department knew better.

'It's not like you to snap at the nurses.'

'I'll apologise to Imogen. I really am fine, things are just busy.'

'It's not just Imogen…' He could tell Heather was uncomfortable with this discussion and he was too. 'I've had a couple of grumbles from staff recently. And we always are busy—especially at this time of year.'

They were. It was a week before Christmas and London was alive. The streets were filled with panicked shoppers, parties, cold weather, ice, families travelling, people meeting. Combine all that with alcohol in abundance and December was always going to be a busy time—only it had never usually fazed him.

'What's going on, Angus?' Heather pushed. 'You just haven't been yourself lately. Look, I know it's not a great time to talk now, but once we get the place settled…or we can catch up for coffee after the shift…'

'Really, I'm fine.' Angus said firmly. Heather was the last person he wanted privy to his problems. Oh, she meant well and everything, but some things were just… private. 'I hate burns, and this one sounds bad.' He gave her a tight smile, picked up the phone when it trilled and spoke to Ambulance Control. Then took another quick drink of water and stood up from his stool. 'They've just got the victim out of the car—ETA twelve minutes…'

For someone who hadn't been shown around, Imogen *had* done a great job of setting up. Burn packs were opened on a trolley, sterile drapes were waiting, and despite his rather abrupt walk out earlier she gave him a roll-of-the-eye smile as Angus returned.

'Couldn't get rid of me, then?'

'Believe me, I tried!' Angus joked, surprisingly refreshed by her humour.

'Given that we're going to be spending the next few hours together, I'd better introduce myself properly— I'm Imogen Lake.'

'Angus…' he offered back, 'Angus Maitlin—I'm one of the consultants here. Look, I'm sorry if I was curt with you earlier.'

'That's OK.'

'No, it's not…' He was washing his hands, but he looked over at her as he spoke. 'I completely jumped the gun—when you said that you'd been pulled from the maternity ward, that you were a midwife, I thought the nursing co-ordinator had messed up.'

'They often do!' She was smiling even more readily now—his rather snooty English accent along with his genuine apology making it very easy to do so.

'You weren't in the middle of a delivery or anything?' Angus asked, wincing just a touch as she nodded.

'And I was enjoying it too.' Imogen added, just to make him feel worse. 'So what do we know about the patient?'

'The victim coming in was the driver of a motor vehicle heading onto the M25.' Angus told her the little he could. 'According to Ambulance Control, the car lost control at the junction, hit the sign and exploded on impact, a fire truck witnessed the whole thing and the crew were straight onto it, putting out the fire as quickly as they could…'

'Is the patient male or female?' Imogen asked.

'We don't know yet.'

'OK.' It was her only response to the grim answer—that the victim's gender hadn't been immediately identified was just another indication of the direness of the situation.

Imogen truly didn't want to be here.

She had spent the last hour in a darkened delivery room, coaching Jamila Kapur through the final first stages of labour and into the second stage. Jamila had just been ready to start pushing when Imogen had been called to the phone.

When the nurse co-ordinator had rung and asked if she'd help out in Emergency, Imogen had immediately said no and not just because she didn't want to go down there. Continuity of care with labouring mums was important to Imogen, and just as she wouldn't have walked out on Mrs Kapur if she had been at that stage of labour when her shift ended, in the same way she hadn't wanted to walk out on her then.

Then the co-ordinator had rung again, reading off her qualifications as if Imogen mightn't be aware that she had them! Telling her that her skills would be better deployed in Emergency and that was where they were sending her.

Her first shift, in a different hospital, in a different country and an agency nurse to boot, she really wasn't in any position to argue.

Imogen felt as if she'd been pulled from the womb herself—hauled from where she had been comfortable and happy then plunged into the bright lights of the busy department, to be greeted by unfamiliar faces, chaos and noise. But—as Imogen always did—she just took a deep breath and decided to get on with it.

It wasn't the patient's fault that she didn't want to be here!

'Where are the gowns?' She answered her own question, pulling two packs down from the rack on the wall. She handed one to Angus before putting on her own, her ample figure disappearing under a mass of shapeless paper, and Angus felt more than a pang of guilt at complaining about her earlier. She seemed completely undaunted by what was coming in, and by all accounts it would be horrific, yet from the organised way she'd set up for the patient, from the qualifications he now knew she had, her unruffled manner wasn't because of ignorance—she was clearly a very experienced nurse.

'The anaesthetist should be here.' Angus glanced at his watch. 'You paged him?'

'Twice.'

On cue he arrived and Imogen handed him a gown too as Angus gave the information they had.

Her fine red hair was already scraped neatly back in a ponytail, but she popped on a paper hat, as Angus did the same, to maintain a sterile field as far as possible and minimise the risk of infection.

The wait was interminable and Angus glanced at his watch, the delay in arrival possibly meaning that the patient had died en route. 'What the hell's keeping—?' His voice stopped abruptly, the short blast of the siren warning of the imminent arrival.

Even though it was still only nine a.m. the sky was so heavy with rain it was practically dark outside. The blue light of the ambulance flashed through the high windows, and Angus gave Imogen a grim smile as they waited those few seconds more. This time, however, her freckled face didn't return it, blonde eyelashes blinking on pale blue eyes as instead she took in a deep breath then let it out as the paramedics' footsteps got louder as they sped their patient towards Resus.

'I hate burns!' Imogen said, catching Angus still looking at her.

It was the only indication, Angus realised, that she was actually nervous.

CHAPTER TWO

IT WAS organised chaos.

The type where everyone worked to save a life—and not just in the emergency department but in so many unseen areas of the hospital. Porters running with vital samples up to Pathology, who in turn raced to give baseline bloods and do an urgent cross-match—as the radiographer came quickly around to take an urgent portable chest film.

The patient's name was Maria. That was all the information they had so far. Her bag carrying all the details that would have identified her had been lost in the furnace of the car. But in a brief moment of consciousness as they had extricated her from the car she had given her name.

The paramedics were dripping wet—a combination of rain, sweat and the dousing of the car, and smelt of petrol and smoke. Their faces were black with soot and dust from the fire. Two of the firefighters were being triaged outside, one with minor burns and one with smoke inhalation.

By every eye-witness account that had been given, Maria should have been dead.

'Core temperature?' Angus snapped as he viewed the young woman in front of him.

'Thirty-four point eight,' Imogen responded.

And it seemed bizarre that someone who had been severely burnt might be suffering from hypothermia, but the dousing, the exposure, the injuries just compounded everything. The thermostat in Resus was turned up, the staff dripping with sweat in the stifling warmth as the patient's burnt body shivered.

'She put up her hands…' Angus was swiftly examining her, and the little bit of hope that had flared in Imogen as they'd wheeled her in was quashed. The beautiful face that she'd first glimpsed was, apart from the palms of her hands and some area on her forearms and buttocks, the only area of her body that wasn't severely burnt.

'TBSA, greater than 85 per cent.' Angus called, and Imogen wrote it down. The total body surface area that had suffered burns was horrific and for now intense Resuscitation would continue. Maria would be treated as any trauma victim, airway, breathing and circulation the first priority, and they would be assessed and controlled before a more comprehensive examination would occur, but things didn't look good. Even though the depth of the burns still needed to be assessed, with every observation, with every revelation the outcome for Maria was becoming more and more dire.

'There was one more victim at the scene—deceased,' the paramedic added quietly. 'No ID.'

'They were in the car together?' Angus checked. 'Is the deceased male or female?' The paramedic gave a tight shake of his head. 'We don't know at this stage. Adult,' he added, which couldn't really be described as consolation, but when the paramedic spoke next, Angus conceded, it was perhaps a small one. 'The child car seat in the rear of the vehicle was empty.'

There were many reasons that no one liked burns—the rapidity, the severity and the potential for appalling injuries, the sheer devastation to the victim's life, the long road ahead, both physically and mentally if they made it through. It took a very special breed of staff indeed to work on a burns unit, and most emergency staff were grateful that they only dealt with this type of injury relatively occasionally and for a short time only.

The golden hour—the hour most critical in determining the outcome for the patient—was utilised to the full for Maria. Despite her appalling injuries, as the fluids were poured in and oxygen delivered, she began to moan.

From the firefighters' accounts and the police officers' initial assessment, the skid marks on the road indicated Maria had struggled desperately to regain control of the car. When it had crashed the nature of her injuries suggested that she had put up her hands instinctively to shield her face, and in doing so she had protected her airway too. Still, she was being closely monitored by the anaesthetist, delivering high-concentration humidified oxygen as well as generous amounts of morphine, ready to intubate earlier rather than later if her airway declined. The paramedics had managed to insert one IV at the scene, but it was insufficient for the volume of fluids required and further access proved impossible.

Instead, Angus delivered the vital fluids she desperately needed via intra-osseous infusion. This was a quick procedure, which needed strength to execute and involved puncturing the bone and delivering the fluids straight into the bone marrow. As Angus did that, Imogen, with great difficulty, inserted a catheter, and watched with mounting unease as Maria's urine output dropped down to zero.

'Can we roll her again?' Angus ordered, and with Heather's help Imogen gently held Maria on her side as Angus, assisted now by a fellow emergency consultant, examined her.

'It's OK, Maria…' Through it all Imogen spoke to her patient, focussing on her face, actually trying not to look at anything else. 'The doctors are just taking a look at you.'

As Maria groaned, Angus nodded and gestured impatiently, telling them they could roll her back. This time neither Heather nor Imogen took any offence at his brusque manner.

'Can I leave you for five minutes?' Heather pulled off her gloves and cursed the ringing phone on the wall and the doctor calling her from the other side of the curtain. 'Press the emergency bell if you need anything at all.'

Now that the patient was relatively more stable, another RN was floating between two patients and assisting where she could, but, for the most part, Imogen was nursing Maria one on one.

Angus now confirmed that most of the burns were full thickness—the most severe kind. It took everything Imogen had to deliver a smile as for the first time and just for a second Maria's eyes briefly opened.

Imogen lowered her head nearer to the patient's. 'It's OK, Maria, you're in hospital, we're looking after you.' It was all she got to say before Maria's eyes closed again.

He'd apologise to Imogen again.

Talking on the telephone to a burns specialist at another major London hospital, and taking a quick swig of water as he did so, Angus looked over and saw Imogen pause for a second to lower her head and talk to the unconscious patient again. She'd done this every couple of minutes or so since Maria had arrived in the department and Angus knew it would be helping as much as the morphine if Maria could hear her.

Angus was proud of the team he had helped build at this hospital, considered them absolutely the best, and yet there was no one who could have done better than Imogen had this morning. Through it all she had been quietly efficient. Everything he had needed had been handed to him and not once had she flinched in assisting Angus in a procedure so vile that even an intern, who had asked to observe had at one point had to walk out.

A vile procedure in a vile, vile morning.

When the burns consultant, Declan Jones, arrived Angus ushered him over to the far wall to discuss the patient privately in greater depth. The stench in the warm room matched the loathsome diagnosis that Angus was just so reluctant to come to.

'I respect your opinion, Declan…' As Imogen walked over to the huddle she could hear the restraint in his voice. 'More than respect it—you know that …'

'She's talking,' Imogen said.

'Is she orientated?' Angus asked, swallowing down a sudden wave of bile.

'Fully. She's Italian, but her English is very good, though she has a strong accent. She's struggling obviously, but she's conscious now. She's confirmed that her surname is Vanaldi. Her husband Rico was the passenger in the car.' He watched those blonde eyelashes blink a couple of times before she continued. 'She has a son called Guido, he's fifteen months old and at day care…'

Till this point information had trickled in in dribs and drabs. The police had managed to ID the vehicle and registration, which had given them an address. They had then been and spoken with neighbours and were now on their way to the day-care centre her child was attending.

'That matches what the police said,' Angus nodded, 'Are there any other relatives we can call?'

'She said not.'

'There must be someone!' Angus insisted, because there just had to be. Maria was a young woman, for goodness' sake, with a child, and she'd just lost her husband. She couldn't be expected to face this alone. 'She needs someone with her.'

'I'll ask her again.'

'Is there any urine output yet?' Angus called as she walked off, his jaw clenching closed when she shook her head.

'Still zero.'

Usually it was good news that the patient was talking. For a patient so ill to now be alert and orientated, in practically every other scenario it would be reason to cheer, but not today.

Maria Vanaldi had awoken probably to be told that she would inevitably die—her calamitous injuries simply incompatible with life.

And it was Angus who would have to be the one to tell her.

'Is there anyone else I can discuss this with?' It was always exquisitely difficult, questioning a colleague, one who actually specialised in the field and whose expertise Angus had called on, but etiquette couldn't really come into it and Declan understood that.

'I'll give you some names.' He let out a sigh. 'Though I've already called two of them. I'm sorry, Angus.'

'There's an older brother,' Imogen stated as a policeman came over, clearly just as drained from it all as the rest of them, and his news wasn't any more cheering.

'We've contacted the day-care centre, they're open till six tonight. The husband's the only other point of contact on their forms.'

'Bring the child to Emergency,' Angus interrupted. 'She'll want to see him and hopefully we'll have some relatives arriving soon.' He turned to Imogen. 'You say that she's got a brother?'

'He's her only relative.' Imogen gave a troubled nod. 'But he's in Italy and Maria doesn't know his phone number. She says it's on her mobile, which is in the car...'

'Can I talk to her?' the police officer asked. 'We can enter the house and go through her phone book or whatever to try and locate the contact number for him, but it would make it quicker if she could tell us where to look.'

Angus shook his head. 'I'll talk to her.'

He approached the bed and smiled into two petrified eyes. 'Hi, Maria, I'm Angus, I'm the doctor looking after you.'

'Guido!'

'Your son?' Angus said. 'He's being taken care of.'

'He's at day care.' In the few minutes since he'd left her side, Maria's degree of consciousness had improved, but even generous amounts of morphine couldn't dim her anguish as adrenaline kicked in and her mind raced to recapture her world. 'He will not know! They will not know…'

'We know where he is,' Angus said gently. 'The police have contacted the day-care centre and are bringing him in here. You'll be able to see him soon.'

'He's not well…' She was choking on her tears, each word a supreme effort. 'He has a cold—I should have kept him at home…'

If only she had, Imogen thought, then checked herself. It was a futile exercise, one patients went through over and over when they or their loved ones landed in Emergency. The recriminations and the reprimands, going over and over the endless, meaningless decisions that had brought them to that point and wishing different choices had been made. As Angus caught her eye for a moment, she knew he was going through it too—if only. If only she had left him at home, or left later, or earlier, or stopped for a chat, or not stopped…

It truly was pointless.

'You couldn't have known,' he said firmly. 'You couldn't have foreseen this. This was not your fault.'

'I wasn't speeding…' And Imogen watched as Maria

thought things through. 'Rico?' Her eyes fled from Angus's to Imogen. 'How is Rico?'

'Who's Rico?'

'My husband.'

'Was he in the car with you?' Angus checked, because he had to.

'How is he?'

And then came the difficult bit, where he had to tell this young woman that there had been another fatality in the car. It was hard when the identity hadn't been confirmed, hard because there was absolutely no point in giving her false hope, and he delivered the brutal news as gently as he could, watching as her shocked, muddled brain attempted to decipher it then chose not to accept it.

'No.' Her denial was followed swiftly by anger, her Italian accent more pronounced, her eyes accusing. 'You've got it wrong. It might not be him.'

'Someone needs to be here for you.' Angus said, choosing not to push it. 'Imogen said you have a brother in Italy. Are there any family or friends closer?'

'Only Elijah.'

'What about Rico's family?'

'No!'

'OK.' She was getting distressed, alarms bleeping everywhere, and he hadn't even told her the hardest part. 'The police are near your house, they can break in and get your brother's phone number. Do you know where it would be?'

'No...' She closed her eyes, swallowed really hard and then gave an answer that only a woman could understand. 'By the phone—but it's a mess.'

'Is it in a phone book?'

'The place is a mess.' Angus frowned just a fraction. People's bizarre responses never ceased to amaze him. Here she was lying in the Resuscitation bay, her husband was dead and she was worried that the house was a mess.

'You should see my place,' Imogen said as she watched Angus's expression, her calm voice reassuring the woman. 'I can promise you that they've seen worse. In fact, I can promise you that they won't even notice the mess. They won't even bat an eyelid.'

It had taken him a moment to get it, but he realised then that it was easier for Maria to focus on the pointless for a moment.

'It's a mess…' The morphine was taking over now, or maybe Maria just didn't care any more as she closed her eyes.

Despite the closed eyes, still Imogen chatted easily to her and Angus could see they had already built up a rapport, which Maria was going to need. 'Just tell me where the number is—his name's Elijah. What's his surname?'

'My surname…' Maria answered.

'Have you got a lot of pain still?' Imogen checked, turning up the morphine pump as soon as Maria nodded wearily. 'We'll keep turning it up till we get on top of it.'

Sometimes, Angus thought to himself, you had to face up to facts. As he desperately did the rounds on the telephone, calling as many people as he knew to ask for a second opinion or for some objective advice, Angus realised that, despite extenuating circumstances, despite supreme effort, despite so much potential and no matter how much he didn't want it to be so, Maria's life would soon fail.

'Her lactate levels alone will kill her.' Imogen met him at the soft-drink machine in the corridor. Heather had taken over for five minutes, giving Imogen a chance to dash to the loo and to get a quick drink. 'You haven't got any change for the machine?' he asked as he ran his hand through his hair.

Imogen emptied her pockets, handing over some coins, and he popped them into the machine, too distracted to ask what she wanted and she too distracted to care. He punched in the same number twice and they gulped icy, fizzy, sweet orange which proved a great choice, sitting in a relatives' interview room for a couple of minutes, before heading back into hell.

'Would you want to know?' Angus looked over to Imogen. 'I want to give her hope—I mean, we'll follow the burns protocol, she'll go up to ICU, but…'

'They moved here from Italy two years ago apparently.' Imogen didn't immediately answer his question. 'The neighbours told the police that they kept themselves pretty much to themselves. They found the brother's number too…' Her voice trailed off as she thought about it, really thought about it, and Angus waited. 'Yes,' she said after the longest time. 'I'd want to know, I'd want to use whatever time I had to make arrangements for my son.'

'Me, too.' He rubbed his hand over his forehead and Imogen could see his agony, could see the compassion behind the rather brusque facade, and knew that this was tearing him up too.

'A little bit of hope is OK, though,' she added.

'There's going to be no Christmas miracle here.'

'I know.' Imogen nodded. 'But Maria's not me and she's not you and if she doesn't want to know…'

'I'll play it by ear.' He stood up, turned to go and then paused. 'Thanks, by the way.' They both knew he wasn't thanking her for the drink. 'I'll go and ring the brother,' Angus said, grateful that she didn't wish him luck, grateful that she just nodded. 'God, I hope he speaks English.'

'I'll send someone to get you if there's anything urgent.'

'Thanks.'

Ringing relatives was never easy and Elijah Vanaldi proved more difficult than most. Hanging up the phone, Angus dragged his hand through his thick mop of hair and held onto it, resting his head in his hand for the longest time, trying to summon the strength to face the *most* difficult part of this vile day: to tell the beautiful, vibrant woman herself that her life would soon be over—that not only had her son lost his father but that, in a matter of, at best, hours, he would lose his mother too.

He flicked off the do-not-disturb light and almost instantaneously someone knocked at the door to his office. Imogen's face was grim as she stepped into the unfamiliar terrain and Angus wondered whether or not it would even be necessary to tell Maria now.

'She knows…' Swallowing hard, Imogen's pale blue eyes met his. 'She knows that she's dying.'

'You told her?' Angus barked, his voice gruff. It was *his* job to do that, and as much as he was dreading it he wanted to ensure that it was done right, but as Imogen shook her head, he regretted his harsh tone.

'Of course I didn't tell her—I'm not a complete idiot!'

And just because they were both snapping and snarling, they knew that there was no need for either of them to say sorry. In the short but painfully long time they'd worked together, they'd already built up a rapport.

'Maria worked it out for herself,' Imogen explained, and he watched as she chewed nervously on her bottom lip for a moment before continuing. 'She said "I'm going to die, aren't I?" And I didn't tell her she was wrong, I simply told her that I'd come and get you to talk to her. I'm just letting you know that she's already pretty much aware…'

'Thank you for telling me.' He gave a weary smile. 'You've been amazing this morning.'

'Not bad for a foreigner?' Imogen gave her own weary smile back, just letting him know that she'd heard all of his earlier complaint to Heather.

'Yes, not bad.' Angus smiled. 'I guess we might have to keep you.'

'How was the brother?' Imogen asked, and neither smiled now.

'Brusque, disbelieving, angry…take your pick. He's on his way.'

'That's good…' Imogen found herself frowning, and couldn't quite work out why. Angus Maitlin had every right to look grim. As gruelling as Emergency was at times, this morning took the cake. Yet she could see the purple stains of insomnia under his eyes, the swallow of nervousness over his perfect Windsor knot, remembered the short fuse he had greeted her with, and knew there had to be more, knew, because she'd been there herself. 'Gus could talk to her…'

'Gus?'

'The other consultant.'

'I know who Gus is,' Angus snapped. 'Don't worry, I can be nice when I remember. Look…' He stopped himself then and forced a half-smile. 'It's just with it being Christmas and everything, my wife's the same age…'

'I know.' Imogen nodded her understanding, but a smudge of a frown remained, not for her patient but for him.

'Come on.' Angus stood up. 'Let's get this over with.'

As they reached the nurses' station, quietly discussing the best way to go about it, Angus became aware that Imogen had more insight into Maria's personality than he did and absorbed her words carefully.

'She's going to be terrified for her little boy, for Guido and his future. I guess the main thing I'd want to hear is that—'

'Angus.' Heather's interruption halted Imogen's train of thought. 'Gemma's on the phone for you.'

'Tell her I'll call her back.'

'She says that it's urgent.'

'It always is with Gemma,' Angus snapped, and Imogen knew that he just wanted to get the unpleasant task of speaking with Maria over with. 'Tell her I'll ring her back when I can.'

'She says that it's to do with the kids.'

'What's the problem, Gemma?'

Imogen frowned as with a hiss of irritation Angus took the telephone. Of course Angus was busy, and of course he didn't want interruptions, but if it had been

Brad ringing to say there was something urgent going on with Heath, Imogen would have been tripping over her feet to get to the phone—no matter how busy she was at work.

'What do you mean—you sacked Ainslie?'

Imogen's glance caught Heather's, and they both shared a slightly wide-eyed look.

'The nanny!' Heather mouthed for Imogen's benefit.

'Oh!'

'The morning I'm having and you ring to tell me you've sacked the nanny. I couldn't give a damn if you've got a photo shoot tomorrow, Gemma.' Pinching the bridge of his nose with his finger and thumb, Angus closed his eyes. 'Frankly, I couldn't have cared less if Ainslie *was* stealing the odd thing—she was the best thing to happen to the kids and to get rid of her one week before Christmas...' He went to hang up then changed his mind. 'No, Gemma, you sort it out for once!'

He aimed the receiver in the general direction of the phone but missed spectacularly, then as he strode towards the Resuscitation area he stopped, dragged in a huge breath and leant against the wall for a moment. Imogen was glad he did, glad he took a moment to compose himself before he went in to see Maria—she deserved calm and his full attention.

'Sorry about that.'

'No problem.' Imogen smiled, because it wasn't. Oh, she didn't have a nanny, of course, but had Brad rung her with something so trivial, she'd have no doubt put on a similar show herself.

'It's just sometimes...' He stopped himself then, just

as she had so many times in another lifetime. And even if she had only just met him, even if they were from opposite sides of the globe and even though he was stunning looking and she was rather, well, plain, Imogen knew that they had one thing in common: both of them had had to work, to function, to keep on keeping on through the rocky part of a failing marriage—even if Angus wasn't ready to admit it.

'Impossible?' she offered, watching his eyes jerk to hers, seeing that flash of surprise that someone might just possibly understand. 'Brad used to ring me all the time with some perceived drama, or I'd be ringing him with one of my own…'

'Brad's your husband?'

'Brad's my ex-husband.'

'Oh!' He pulled away from the wall then, clearly deciding that she didn't understand at all, that the flash of recognition that he'd thought he'd seen actually didn't apply to him in the slightest.

'It isn't actually a *perceived* drama,' he said tartly. 'Gemma was right to ring, she just caught me at a bad time.'

'Sure.'

'Really,' he insisted. 'Gemma and I are fine. It just wasn't the best time to call, that's all.'

'Good.'

He was about to insist again that nothing was wrong, but Imogen decided it wasn't her business anyway, the fleeting moment of connection long since gone. It was time now to get on with the unpleasant task in hand— and it was Imogen who concluded the conversation.

'Let's go and speak with Maria.'

CHAPTER THREE

IMOGEN HAD nursed since the age of eighteen, and now at thirty-two years of age and with most of her experience in either Intensive Care or Emergency, she had seen more than her fair share of tragedy and dealt with many unbearably sad situations. Most stayed with her enough to be recalled when required, some would stay with her for ever—and some, like Maria, would actually change her.

Despite his cool greeting and sometimes brusque demeanour, still Imogen had liked Angus. She had worked in Emergency long enough to form a very rapid opinion, and generally she was spot on.

And now, listening to him confirm Maria's darkest fears, Imogen knew that she was right. Understood even why he wanted to be the one to tell her. Lacing compassion with authority, he led her through the news, tender yet firm he let her find her own route, which was, for Maria, to face the truth. When many others would have left, Angus stayed, reiterating when needed and sometimes just quiet as Maria had to grieve for her own short life too. Yet somehow she rallied, maternal instinct kick-

ing in, knowing that in the little time that remained she had to make plans for her son.

'I have to speak to my brother.' Her blue eyes were urgent. 'I cannot die before I speak with him.'

'He said the same thing,' Angus said gently. 'He's flying in.'

'I need to speak to him about Guido —about what must happen to him.'

'I'll also get Social Services to come and speak to you—' Angus started, but Maria was having none of it.

'I just want Elijah.'

'Do you have a will, a lawyer?' Angus asked, but Maria simply wouldn't go there. Her brother was the only one she would consider talking to, the only person she wanted now apart from her son.

'Your brother's on his way,' Angus said.

'How long does a flight take from Rome to London?' Imogen asked.

'About three hours,' Angus answered, but there was also getting to the airport, booking a flight and realistically they were looking more at five or six hours, and no one was sure Maria had that.

'I think I want to see Guido.' Maria screwed up her eyes with the agony of it. 'But I'm worried that I'll scare him…'

'Your face is fine,' Imogen said softly. 'I'll give it a wash and we'll make sure everything else is covered. I'll turn down all the machines so that they don't alarm him.'

'I won't be able to hold him,' Maria croaked.

'I'll hold him for you,' Imogen said. 'I'll put his face right next to yours and you can feel him and smell him…'

'I don't want to start crying. I don't know if I want him to see me like this.'

'OK,' Imogen soothed. 'You let me know.'

'How's her pain?' Angus checked a little while later. Maria was calmer, lying with her eyes closed but not sleeping as Imogen sat quietly by her side.

'I'm OK.' She opened her eyes to let Angus know she wasn't sleeping. 'Any word from my brother?'

'Not yet.'

'Then I'll wait.'

'Don't try and be brave,' Imogen said. 'We can keep increasing your morphine, make you more comfortable…'

'No more till Elijah is here—I want to be conscious when my brother comes.'

Imogen had long since learnt that people were people, women still women even in the most dire of times—even when they were dying. Friends and just a bit of a smile were always needed. Suddenly Maria was asking for her face to be washed and if she could be tidied up a bit—as she emotionally prepared herself to see her son. A healthy dose of morphine combined with a good measure of denial meant that Maria managed a little chat as Imogen gently tended to her.

'I forgot to bring my make-up.' It took a second to realise that Maria had managed a joke and they shared a smile. 'I am never without it.'

'I've got some lipstick,' Imogen offered, 'if you want to use it.'

'Thank you. You know, I thought I was imagining things when I saw Angus.'

'I thought I was, too, when I came on duty,' Imogen grinned, glad to be Maria's friend today, glad that for a little while more Maria could be Maria. 'Bloody gorgeous, isn't he?'

'He's on the television, too.' Maria said, her eyes almost crossed as she tried to focus.

'Angus?' Imogen frowned.

'A lot—he's a TV doctor or something.'

'I'll have to remember to set my DVD to record him.' Imogen winked. 'A little memento to take back to Australia. Hey…' Imogen frowned for the first time at her patient. 'How come your eyeliner's still on?'

'It's a tattoo!' Maria coughed as she tried to laugh.

'Wow!' Imogen was genuinely impressed. 'I've always wanted to get my eyelashes dyed—I've just never got around to it.'

'Do it!' Maria said, managing to focus her eyes on Imogen. 'Go and do it!'

'I will.'

'Have a proper break.' Heather was insistent. 'I'll go in and stay with her. I want you to go and have a coffee and a sandwich and catch your breath for a little while. You, too!' Heather added to Angus.

There really was no point being a martyr—Imogen had learnt that long ago. Sure, there were times when ten minutes for a quick drink and a sit-down *were* impossible to find, but today Imogen knew that a quick refuel would help not just the doctor and nurse but the patient too. Maria was being reviewed by the anaesthetist now, the team ensuring that everything possible was being done to keep Maria pain free and to respect her wishes to remain conscious for as long as possible until her brother arrived.

Peeling off the dirty gowns and paper hats, it was a relief to be out of them. Imogen was aware she must look a sight, her red hair damp with sweat and stuck to her head. Looking at Angus, there was no doubt that she too had a nice big crease around her forehead where her hat had been, only her uniform, she was sure, wasn't quite as fresh looking as his crisp shirt.

And though she had joked with Maria about it, now that she was alone with him, away from the horrors, for the first time Imogen *really* noticed how gorgeous he was.

His beautifully cut hair had recovered from the cap just a little better than hers, and as she walked behind him to the staffroom she saw how it tapered into his neck, saw the wide set of his shoulders and caught a whiff of his gorgeous scent as he held the door open and they walked inside. He was so tall and broad he actually made Imogen feel slender as she stood beside him and loaded four slices of bread into the toaster and he made two quick coffees. He had nice hands too, Imogen thought, noticing how he stirred sugar into her coffee. But seeing his wedding band glint, she chose not to go there.

Wouldn't do to others what had been done to her— not that a man as divine as Angus Maitlin would even deign her that sort of a glance!

Still, he wasn't just nice to look at, he was a nice guy too, and after the morning they'd so far shared, it was nice to actually *meet* him.

And it felt so-o-o good to sit down.

So good not to be in that room where death was present. So good that, despite the horrors, despite the fact it was the foremost thing on both their minds, for most of their break they chose not to talk about it.

'So you're from Australia?'

'Queensland.' Imogen nodded.

'And you only just got here.'

'I didn't intend to start work quite so quickly. I was supposed to be finding somewhere to stay, but when I checked into the youth hostel there were already four messages from the hospital asking if I could ring them—I'd sent in all my paperwork and references a few weeks ago.'

'So what brings you here?' Angus asked. She didn't look like the regular travellers they got here—young nurses just qualified and ready to party. His eyes narrowed as he tried to guess her age—late twenties, early thirties perhaps. 'You said you've got a son?'

'I do…' He watched as her face brightened. 'Heath. He's here with his dad. Brad's working in London, so I thought I'd come over for Christmas.'

Angus's narrowed eyes were joined by a frown now and he fought quickly to check it. So what if her child lived on the other side of the world with his father? It certainly wasn't his place to judge.

'I was hoping to work just a couple of nights a week to cover the rent in a serviced apartment,' Imogen continued, 'but having seen the prices of temporary rentals that I *can* afford…' Imogen pulled a face. 'Well, let's just say they're not exactly the places I'd want to bring Heath back to! So it looks like I'm going to just have to take him sightseeing when I see him.'

'You're separated from your husband?' Angus checked.

'Divorced.'

'And he's English?'

'He's Australian.' Imogen laughed, enjoying his confusion. 'Brad's just working here.'

'So what does he do for a living? If you don't mind me asking.'

'He's an actor!' Imogen rolled her eyes. 'And not a very good one either—if you don't mind me saying.' Angus's frown was replaced by a grin as she smiled at him.

'Maria said that you're on television too!'

'She recognised me?' He could feel his cheeks redden. It was the one thing in his life that embarrassed him. He took his television appearances seriously, saw it as an excellent means for education, but lately personal questions had been creeping into the show, a sort of thirst for knowledge about him was being created, a celebrity status evolving that, unlike Gemma, he didn't aspire to. 'I have a regular spot on a current affairs show, discussing current medical trends, health issues... It's no big deal.'

'It is to Maria! She thinks you're marvellous!' Imogen winked. 'Says you're quite a hottie.'

'A hottie?' Angus queried then wished he hadn't, working it out before Imogen could answer.

'Cute!' Imogen grinned. 'But, I told her the camera *always* lies, and given I was married to an actor for years. I speak on good authority.' He couldn't quite make her out. She was very calm, laid back even, but she had this dry edge to her humour he liked.

'Anyway...' Angus went to bite into his toast '...I'm going to give it up soon.'

'Had enough?' Imogen said casually, but Angus, though apparently calm, was actually reeling inside! He hadn't told anyone that, had only *just* broached the subject with Gemma. It was just the sort of careless comment that he shouldn't be making. He hadn't even told them at the show, and he moved quickly to right it.

'I'd rather you didn't say anything.'

'About what?' Imogen asked.

'About what I just said.' Angus cleared his throat. 'It wouldn't look good if it got out.'

'I'll say!' Imogen grinned. 'We can't have everybody knowing that the amazing Dr Maitlin doesn't even know what a hottie is!'

In a morning where there should have been none, somehow she'd brought just a touch of laughter, and not just to him, Angus noticed, but to their patient too. Imogen Lake, the only shred of good fortune Maria Vanaldi had had today.

Emergency's gain, Maternity's loss, Angus thought, thinking back to his obstetric rotation. She'd be great at that too.

'So you're a midwife too?'

'I am.' But suddenly she wasn't quite so forthcoming.

'You're emergency trained, though—clearly!'

'Yes.'

'And Heather said you had ICU qualification,' Angus pushed. 'So which do you prefer?'

'I don't know. I've been doing emergency for years now—since I qualified. I love it and everything, but...'

He watched as she shrugged. 'Midwifery never really appealed to me till I had Heath. I've kept my hand in and I generally do a shift a month at the birthing centre at the local maternity hospital back home. I'm thinking of applying for a full-time job there when I get back. Actually…' she gave a tight smile '…I'm thinking about a lot of things.'

'Won't you miss Emergency?'

'That's a bit of a daft question to ask this morning,' she answered, and Angus would have loved to have spoken to her some more, was actually sorry when the quick reprieve was over when she drained her cup and stood. 'Speaking of which, I'd better get back to Maria.'

'I'll be there in a moment.'

'Thank you—' Maria held Imogen's eyes '—for being there today. I'm so glad it was you.'

'I'm glad it was me too…' Imogen answered, and even though today had been one of the worst shifts in memory and she'd have given anything to have missed it, would far rather have been bringing a gorgeous life into the world than helping one come to an end, somehow she was glad she had been there too, because she had helped. Imogen felt safe in the knowledge that she had done her job well—and Maria deserved that today.

She was a good nurse—Imogen knew that—and a good woman too, and today Maria had needed both. As painful as it might be, Imogen was actually glad that she *could* help this woman on her final journey.

'I don't want to die!' Loaded with morphine now,

Maria's eyes were like pinpricks as she tried to focus on Imogen.

'I know.' Imogen stroked her cheek.

'I'm not ready.'

'I know.'

She could feel Angus, fiddling with the morphine, checking Maria's NG tube, lifting up the catheter and checking that there was still no output, and Imogen knew somehow that he was there for her. And as Imogen removed her mask, knowing it was pointless now, she felt him in the room as she did the hardest bit of nursing and gave a bit more of herself to her patient.

'I'm scared.'

And she could say I know again, only Imogen knew she had to give more, had to ask her patient for more, and Angus's hand on her shoulder was very gratefully received. The stab of his fingers in her shoulder actually hurt a touch as they dug in, but they were very welcome––that someone was standing silently beside her, supporting her as she tried to support Maria and tie up the loose knots in a life about to be taken too soon.

'What are you most scared of, Maria?' Imogen asked, because until she knew she couldn't possibly understand the most vital bits in Maria's life. 'Tell me and if I can help I will.'

'I'm scared for Guido. I'm scared that Rico's family will get him…' Maria screwed her eyes closed. 'Elijah knows.'

'Your brother?' Imogen checked.

'He knows what they're like. I don't want them raising him.'

'What about your brother?' Imogen asked. 'Can he raise Guido?'

'I don't know…' Maria sobbed. 'I don't know if he can, if he'll want to. He doesn't have children, he's not married… I need to talk to him. He knows how it is…' Maria's eyes pleaded for understanding that Imogen failed for a second to give, but thankfully there was a man behind her who stepped right in.

'Elijah will be here soon.' Still Angus gripped her shoulder as he spoke. 'And I promise you that we will come up with the very best solution we can for your son.'

Elijah rang his sister from the plane, and Imogen held the telephone while Maria spoke to him, but it was too much for Maria, sobbing into the phone despite her brother's attempts to calm her.

'She's getting more distressed…' Imogen took over the call, speaking to the man whose Italian accent was thick and rich. He sounded incredibly together, given the circumstances, but Imogen could hear the pain behind each word. 'She just needs to see you. I know you're doing your best to get here.'

There were no thank yous or goodbyes from either of them, nothing the other could say, both just dealing with it the best that they could.

Maria's condition continued to worsen, so much so that when Elijah rang again to check on his sister and to say that his plane would be landing soon it was becoming ever clearer that he might not get here in time. Angus wearily closed his eyes for a second before he began speaking on the phone. Maria was sobbing in earnest now, scared to see Guido and scared not to, and finally Imogen made the decision for her.

'You need to see your baby.' Imogen said softly. 'I'll go to the ward and get him.'

'Will you stay with me?'

'Of course…' Imogen soothed.

'Not just while I'm with Guido… Till Elijah…'

'Of course,' Imogen said again, because she would.

'Are you OK?' Angus asked as Imogen blew her nose at the nurses' station. She was waiting to be put through to the charge nurse on the children's ward to say that she was coming up to fetch Guido.

'Not really.'

'Do you want me to ask Heather if she can swap nurses? You've been in with Maria for ages, it must be—'

'I don't think Maria needs a fresh face appearing at the moment.'

'If it gets too much…' Angus offered, but she just rolled her eyes and the conversation was terminated as the charge nurse on the children's ward came to the phone and offered to bring him down herself. But Imogen declined.

'I'll come and get him. I'm going to hold him while he sees her, so it might be better if I introduce myself to him up there on the ward.'

First, though, she went back into Maria to let her know that she'd see Guido very soon then arranged cotton sheets around Maria to hide the worst of her burns.

'How do I look?' Maria managed a brave feeble joke.

'Like his mum,' Imogen said gently. 'He'll cry because of the machinery, not you. Your face is fine.'

* * *

Guido didn't cry, just whimpered to get closer to his mum, and Imogen held him carefully, doing her utmost not to cry herself as Maria, aching for contact, pressed her cheek against her son and told him she loved him over and over. Even Angus was glassy-eyed when he came in to check on her, and finally when it was too much for Guido, when his mum wasn't holding him as he wanted, when the pain and emotion were just too much for Maria, Imogen made the horrible decision and took Guido back up to the children's ward, treating Guido as she could only hope someone would treat Heath if the roles had been reversed.

Stepping into the children's ward was like stepping into Santa's grotto—reindeer pulling sleighs lined the walls, snowflakes were sprayed on the windows and a wonderful tree glittered behind barriers at the nurses' station, only they didn't put a smile on Imogen's face.

Dangerously close to tears, irritated by the nurses' chatter at the desk, she told them that she was back and walked to Guido's room. He was too confused to cry now, the police, the hospital, his mum, these strangers all too much. Utterly exhausted and bewildered, Guido almost jumped out of her arms and into the metal hospital cot, clinging to a teddy bear, curling up like a little ball and popping his thumb in his mouth. Imogen quietly stroked his hair as his eyes closed and waited till he was asleep before heading back down to Maria.

As Imogen stepped back into Emergency she was greeted by a Santa Claus being pushed on an ambulance trolley and writhing in pain. 'Strangulated hernia—

where do you want him?' the paramedic said, trying his best to sound serious.

'I'll take him.' Heather grinned. 'You're finished now, Imogen.'

Imogen glanced at her watch, surprised to see that it was already nearly one o'clock—the end of her shift. 'What's happening with Maria?'

'She's going up to ICU. They just rang to say they're ready.'

'I'll take her up,' Imogen offered. 'I'll go and get my time sheet. Just sign me off for one.'

'Imogen…' Angus called her as she headed out of the doors with Maria. Security was holding a lift for her, and the porters had sent an extra person along to ensure that the path was clear for a speedy run up to ICU. It really wasn't a ideal time to stop for a chat.

'Thanks for this morning.'

'No problem.'

'No, really, Heather or I should go over it with you. Come back down after ICU—'

'I don't have time.' Imogen shook her head.

'You have to make time.' Angus pushed.

'Really, I'm fine.' Imogen said, gesturing to the porters to get going, and there really wasn't much else Angus could say.

Speeding along the corridor and then handing over the patient to the ICU staff, Imogen sat down beside Maria, not as a nurse this time but as a friend.

At least until Elijah got here.

CHAPTER FOUR

WITH his entire day almost taken up with Maria Vanaldi, by the time his patient was wheeled up to ICU, a lot of things had piled up for Angus.

And not just at work.

Grabbing a coffee, he headed to his office for five minutes to ring Gemma, hoping that whatever the latest crisis was to blow up at home, it had somehow been diverted. 'Hey, Gemma.' He heard the cold silence of her answer, but still tried. 'Sorry about before and taking so long to get back to you—it's been hell here.'

'Well, it's not exactly been a barrel of laughs here!'

'We had this woman in,' Angus attempted. 'She's the same age as you, her husband died, they've got a toddler…' Only he could tell she didn't want to hear it, which made it impossible to share it. Oh, he knew he couldn't take it all home and, yes, it annoyed him too when she droned on and on about her own career, but sometimes he listened, sometimes he tried, and he really needed her to at least try today.

It just wasn't going to happen.

'Can we talk about *your* family for a moment, please, Angus?'

He didn't bother to tell her that he'd been trying to.

Instead he heard, rather sharply, how they were still minus a nanny a week before Christmas and how Gemma *had* to work tomorrow. And if there wasn't already enough to deal with, there was something else gnawing at Angus.

'It just doesn't make any sense. I can't believe that Ainslie would steal.'

'She's got money problems,' Gemma pointed out. 'Ainslie told you about that loan she had with her ex-boyfriend, well, maybe it was starting to catch up…'

'None of that was her fault, though.'

'Angus, whose side are you on here? I caught the nanny stealing—what the hell did you want me to do? Give her a pay rise?'

Frankly, yes! he was tempted to answer, if it avoided all this!

'So where is she now?' Angus asked instead.

'I don't know and I don't care,' Gemma huffed. 'She's hardly our responsibility.'

But to Angus she was.

Ainslie had been with the family for three months now. She had lined up the job with his family from her home in Australia and though at twenty-eight years old she wasn't some naive teenager, he didn't like the idea of her being kicked out onto the street with no money, no reference and just a week before Christmas. She was way too old to be his daughter, but if, heaven forbid, Clemmie ever loaded up a backpack and headed to the other side of the world, he could only hope that some-one, somewhere, would feel equally responsible.

Just as he did now.

And not just for Ainslie.

Imogen was from Australia, had landed here just a day or so before and had walked into a nursing shift from hell. In mid-conversation with his wife, Angus watched the red light on his phone flash, indicating that someone else was trying to get through, then his pager began to beep and the balls that Angus juggled, as he always did, suddenly all paused in mid-air.

Just this tiny pregnant pause as for a second every-thing just seemed to stand still.

Gemma's voice came as though from somewhere way in the distance as whoever it was on the other line gave up and the red light went off. Angus snapped off his pager before the second shrill and there was just still-ness as the only thing on his mind was the woman he had worked with that morning. He could see her so clearly it was as if she was standing in front of him, those pale blue eyes blinking back at him, her freckly, kind face full of understanding, and he knew that she knew.

Knew, even though he'd denied it, that for him things were hell right now.

'Angus.' Gemma's voice snapped him to weary atten-tion. 'You're going to have to take the day off tomorrow or ring your mother and ask her to come down. I simply cannot miss this shoot—you know how important—'

'Gemma…' His voice was supremely calm, but there was an edge to it, enough of an edge to tell Gemma that she'd better listen carefully. 'We've got more important things to worry about than a photo shoot, or whether or not I come in to work tomorrow, or finding a new nanny. Yes, I will see if I can get cover for tomorrow, but not so that you can go on your photo shoot. I'm going to ask my sister to watch the kids and then…' He took a deep breath and made himself say it '…we need to do some serious talking.'

'Hey!' Lost in thought, Angus nearly collided with Imogen as he headed for the staff lockers. 'I thought you finished ages ago?'

'I did!' Imogen nodded. 'I just didn't like to leave Maria on her own. I know the ICU nurses are fab and everything but, well, I got to talk to her, I guess I was there when she first came in, it just seemed wrong to leave her…'

'How about a drink? I'm sure I owe you one.'

'No thanks.'

'I can have a word with Heather,' Angus offered. 'I'm happy to speak to Admin about your hours…'

'I sat down all afternoon.' Imogen gave a watery smile. 'I made it very clear to the ICU nurses that I was there as a friend for Maria and nothing else. I don't want to be paid for it.'

'How is she?' Angus said slowly. He'd been asked to be kept informed but, given Imogen was here, he wondered if he was just about to hear the news they all expected.

'Not good. Her brother arrived half an hour ago. She's spoken to him, but she's starting to get distressed…' Imogen's eyes filled up, 'I brought Guido in again and she's had a good dose of morphine. The anaesthetist is going to intubate her soon. To be honest, I couldn't take it much more.'

'What will you do now?' Angus asked, not that it was his concern, of course, but he was worried about her, knew the toll today would have taken on her. The thought of going back to the cheerful, carefree world of a youth hostel certainly wouldn't appeal to him today and he doubted it would appeal to Imogen.

'I don't know.' She gave a tight shrug, blew her fringe skywards, and then said it again. 'I don't know.'

'Maybe see your son…' Angus suggested, though it wasn't his place, but with what she'd had to endure today, with all that she'd taken on, it was surely right that he was concerned, surely right that he didn't want her heading off alone. 'Do you talk to your ex?'

'Not about important things.' She gave a tight smile. 'I'll be fine.'

'Look, maybe—' Angus's voice stopped as quickly as it had started. The most stupid idea had come to mind, that maybe she could stay with him and Gemma for a few weeks, help out with the kids while Gemma went on her shoot and while they found a new nanny, but as her eyes darted to his, for reasons he didn't even want to fathom, he quickly changed his mind. 'Come and have a coffee—I've got time.'

'No, you haven't.'

'You're right,' Angus admitted. 'But I'm already so far behind today that I'm never going to catch up. Have a drink…'

'I'd really rather not…' She gave a pale smile. 'I'm not very good company.'

'I don't expect good company.' He frowned at her pale face and lips and was really quite worried now. 'You need a debrief, Imogen. I make sure our regular staff get to talk things through when there's been a difficult patient. It's hard enough for them, never mind agency staff, especially ones who have just landed in the country…'

'I'm fine.' She wouldn't accept his smile and she wouldn't accept his help. Except she wasn't fine, tears were filling those pale blue eyes now, the tip of her snub nose red, and all Angus knew was that he didn't want her to go, didn't want her heading off onto the wet London streets, with no one to unload to. 'How about you?'

'Me?' Her question confused him. They were supposed to be talking about her!

'This morning didn't upset you?'

'Of course it did, but I'm used to it—it's a busy hospital…'

'You can never get used to that.' She shook her head. 'I've been doing this for years and, believe it or not, we do get our fair share of trauma in Australia, even the occasional burn. But *that*, by anyone's standards, was awful.'

'Yes.' Angus admitted. 'It was.'

'So?' She demanded. 'Who debriefs the boss?'

'I get by…' Angus shrugged. 'I speak to the other consultants sometimes and Heather's pretty good. Mind you, I try not to…' His voice trailed off for a moment. 'Well—as you said, I'm the boss.'

'What about your wife?'

A short, incredulous laugh shot out of his lips before

he could stop it and it was all evident in his bitter, mirth-less laugh.

'You're fine too, then?' Her ironic words were the kindest, most honest he'd heard in a long time and Angus stood there. They both just stood there for the longest time, the moment only broken when Heather walked past.

'Oh, there you are Angus. There's a baby I'm moving over to Resus—not quite sure what's going on but very listless…' She gave Imogen a kind, tired smile. 'I'm glad to see you, Imogen. I was actually going to ring you. ICU just called—Maria's just passed away. Her brother wanted to thank you both for all you did for her…'

There was a long silence. Heather bustled off, Angus telling her he'd be there in just a moment, and still he stood and watched as a fat tear slid down Imogen's cheek and she quickly wiped it away with the back of her hand. Angus cursed how times had changed, how it was im-possible these days to comfort a colleague with a quick cuddle, unless it was one you really knew well, as it could so easily be construed as inappropriate. He didn't even have a hanky to offer her, just a paltry 'I'm sorry'.

'She was never going to live…' Imogen sniffed and then wept just a little bit more, before pulling herself together. 'Told you I hated burns,' she said, hitching up her bag up and wishing him a good evening.

Inappropriate. As Angus checked over the baby, as he listened to its chest, checked the depressed fontanel, took bloods and started an IV, his mind was completely on the job, but later, filling out the lab forms and waiting to be put through to Pathology, his mind wandered back to

Imogen. Oh, yes, it *would* have been inappropriate to hold her—because it wouldn't have just been about work.

The last year of his marriage had, by mutual agreement with his wife, been a loveless, sexless pit, but not once had he been tempted. Oh, sure, there had been offers and he wasn't blind enough not to notice a beautiful woman, only Imogen wasn't a classic beauty, Imogen wasn't his type at all.

But, then, what was his type?

God, but he'd wanted to hold her...

He actually shook his head as he sat there. He wasn't going to go there—even in his head. They'd shared the shift from hell, there was bound to be some sort of connection between them and anyone would be worried about her heading off alone. But even after speaking to Pathology and hanging up the phone, despite not a single rustle of paper, as he sat there Angus could feel the winds of change whistling through the department. He could feel the unsettling breeze swirling around him and knew, just knew, that things couldn't go on the way they were.

CHAPTER FIVE

'HI THERE!'

Walking through the car park, cursing the snow that had started to fall, lost in thought, dread in every cell of his body and grey with tension, Angus did a double-take as the vibrant woman greeted him.

Oh, my! was his first thought.

She should never wear white! was his second.

Wearing long, flat black boots, black stockings, black skirt and the softest grey jumper under a cropped black jacket, Imogen was somehow a blaze of colour with her red hair. There was a rosy tinge to her pale cheeks and those once fair eyelashes were now black too, a slick of mascara bringing out the blue of her eyes, and her soft smiling mouth was certainly pretty in pink.

'Sorry,' Angus blinked, 'I didn't recognise you without your uniform. How are you?'

'Great.' She smiled. 'Well, I'm starting to get over my jet-lag anyway! I just popped in to Admin to hand in my time sheet—I forgot yesterday. Oh, and I nipped in to see Mrs Kapur.'

'Mrs Kapur?' Angus frowned.

'She had a little girl, six pounds four and doing beautifully. She even let me have a little hold!'

'That's right, you were in the middle of a delivery…'
Now the surprise at seeing her out of uniform was rapidly wearing off, Angus regretted prolonging the conversation. He had merely been trying to be polite, but now all Angus wanted to do was head into Emergency and do what he had to. He really didn't want to be standing in a car park, making idle chit-chat, only Imogen didn't appear to be in a hurry to go anywhere.

'How were things when you got home?'

'Fine.' Angus nodded and moved to go, before politeness forced him to ask, 'How about you?'

'Well, I'd hardly call the youth hostel home. I lasted about twenty minutes!'

She *had* been great yesterday, Angus reminded himself, and like him would have had had no one to talk to about it so it would be rude now to cut her off, not to ask the question she was waiting for.

'So, what did you do?'

'I went and got my eyelashes dyed and then took a gentle spin on the London Eye and cried my eyes out. I must have looked a fright! I'm surprised the other passengers didn't press the emergency bell. What about you?'

'Me?'

'How are you?'

'I told you, I'm…' He was just about to make the usual polite response that meant nothing, just about to move on and get on with his day, but something stopped him. Whether it was the events of the last few hours that had him acting out of character, or whether it was her that made him change his mind, Angus wasn't sure and could hardly believe he said the words that slipped out of his grim mouth. 'Well, since you ask, I'm feeling pretty crap actually!'

And still she smiled, still she didn't move, just blinked those newly dyed eyelashes back at him and stared at him with those blue eyes. There were bits of snow in her hair now, Angus thought, one flake on her eyelashes, and just this…something. Something that made him stand there, that made him speak when perhaps he shouldn't, made the morning's events real when till now it had felt like a bad dream.

'My marriage just broke up.'

'Just?' A smudge of a frown was the only change to her expression.

'About four hours ago…' What the hell was he doing? Here he was standing in the car park and telling an agency nurse his problems, yet it was as if a ticker-tape parade was coming out of his mouth! Words just spilling out! All he could do was wait for the procession to pass as it all tumbled out. 'I'm just about to go into work—tell them I can't come in over the next few days. I've no idea who's going to fill in for me over Christmas…'

'How are the kids?' She dragged his mind back to the important part of the problem.

'My sister's watching them.'

'They're not with their mum?'

'No, she's gone.' She was frowning now and Angus didn't like it. He neither needed nor wanted her concern.

'She's just gone?'

'It's all under control!' Angus snapped, only it wasn't. He had a horrible feeling that there was a tinge of panic in his voice, it sure as hell sounded like it. He was an emergency consultant, for heaven's sake, was used to dealing with drama and problems, only it wasn't that his marriage was over that had him reeling—he'd dealt with that ages ago. No, now it was the thought of facing the kids, of telling them—what? He didn't know.

'Come and have a coffee.'

Was that her answer? Was she mad?

Angus certainly looked at her as if she was!

'I don't have time…' He didn't. He had to go into work and give them the news that the dependable Angus, one of only two emergency consultants covering the Christmas break, actually couldn't cover it. The thought of sitting in the canteen or the staffroom and talking, instead of doing, was incomprehensible.

'Come on…' She gestured with her head, and started to walk away from the hospital, offering the same wise words he had offered yesterday. 'You have to make time.'

'I don't have sugar…' Irritated, but not at her, he snapped out the words. His life was down the drain, he had a million things he *had* to get on with, yet here he was sitting in a packed café, surrounded by Christmas shoppers. Carols were frying his brain from the speakers overhead as she calmly came over with two big mugs of sickly, milky coffee and proceeded to load them with sugar.

'You do today.' Imogen shrugged as a strange sort of grin came to her lips. 'You're in shock!'

'Shut up!' He actually laughed. On a day when he

never thought he would, when there was nothing, not a single thing to smile about, he started to laugh. Maybe he *was* in shock, Angus thought. Maybe this strange euphoria, this sort of relief that was zipping into him, was some sort of shock reaction, which a mug of something hot and sweet wasn't ever going to cure. But, as he took a sip, it somehow did. Not a lot, not even a little bit, but it sort of did do something.

'I'm not in shock,' he said finally when he'd taken a drink and put down his mug, 'because it really wasn't a shock—I just didn't think it would be today that it ended.'

'And certainly not the day after she sacked the nanny.' Imogen, as she always seemed to, Angus was realising, got right to the very point. 'How old are your children?'

'Jack's five, Clemmie's four.'

'Are they at school?'

'Jack is.' He nodded. 'Clemmie starts in September. Not that it makes any difference at the moment, they're on holiday and I'm rostered on all over Christmas. She sacked our cleaning lady last month as well,' Angus added gloomily. 'The house is like a bomb site!'

'Can you ask her to come back?' Imogen asked.

'Who—Gemma or the cleaning lady?'

'The nanny.' Imogen grinned, assessing him as she would a patient and glad to see he had his sense of humour intact.

'Don't think so…' He shook his head. 'I went to see her this morning; I gave her her holiday money and a reference. She's actually already found another job— you'll never guess who for.'

'Who?' Imogen frowned.

'Guess.'

'I don't know anyone in London.'

'Guido!' He watched as her jaw dropped. 'As dire as my situation is, I think Maria's brother needs help more than I do right now—and Ainslie's great. It's good to know that Guido's being taken care of.'

'By a thief?' Imogen pointed out.

'No.' Angus took a long drink of his coffee. 'I'm pretty sure that I was right about that too…' He gave a tight smile as she sat there bemused. 'And I'd hazard a guess that the cleaning lady wasn't guzzling our gin either.'

'You've lost me.'

'Never mind. My loss is Elijah Vanaldi's gain…' Angus said evasively, 'that's all you need to know. Guido will be well taken care of by Ainslie.'

'So what happened?' Imogen asked. 'With you and Gemma?'

He gave a tight smile. He certainly wasn't going to go there—and certainly not with a stranger. 'I'm sure you'll understand, given that you've been through it yourself, if I don't want to talk about it.'

'No.' Imogen shook her head. 'Talking about it is the only way to get through it.'

'For you perhaps,' Angus clipped, but Imogen wasn't fazed.

'I'll show you mine if you show me yours.'

Why was he grinning again?

'Brad had an affair.'

'I'm sorry.'

'Oh, no.' Imogen gave him a startled look. 'Don't be sorry—it was absolutely my fault!'

'Pardon?'

'He had needs, you see…' Imogen said. 'Very Special Needs. He's very good-looking, he's an actor, you know…'

'Oh.'

'I mean, what was I thinking, Angus?' She shot him a serious look. 'I should have been at the gym if I'd cared about him, really cared about him. I'd have lost my weight straight after I had Heath, now, wouldn't I? And I certainly wouldn't have had a baby guzzling on my boobs at all hours of the night. I would have asked about his day more, wouldn't I, Angus?'

She was like icy water on an impossibly hot day, just this refreshing drench that stunned him. He didn't get her, yet he was starting to want to—never knew when she opened her mouth where it was going, yet every word gave him something, like this join-the-dot picture, as she revealed herself.

'If I had really wanted to keep him,' she continued, not lowering her voice, not caring who might hear, just utterly at ease with herself she carried on. He was half smiling, but very sad too as he stared at this amazing woman— sad for all she had been through, but smiling at the way she shared it. 'I would have stroked his ego more, I would have been tidier, remembered to put on my make-up before he came home, perhaps dressed a bit better. You see, Angus, I didn't understand how demanding his career was, but *she* did. *She* appreciated him, she understood his Very Special Needs—whereas I was fat, lazy and lousy in bed!' She ticked them off one by one on her hands. 'So, you see, it was absolutely my fault that he had an affair.'

'I'm sorry.'

'For what?'

'For what you must have been through. I'm sure you didn't deserve it.'

'I didn't,' Imogen said without even a trace of bitterness. 'And I'm not, by the way!'

'Not what?'

'Fat.'

'No,' Angus politely agreed, 'you're not.'

'I mean, I'm not supermodel material—I accept that—and, yes, I do like to eat, but I think there are better words to describe me than fat!'

'You're not fat.' Obviously getting hot now, she'd taken off her jacket, big boobs jiggling under her jumper. Her skirt was biting into her waist over her soft, round tummy, and Angus felt a terribly inappropriate stirring under the table. 'You're…' *Gorgeous* was what he'd been about to say, but that seemed too much. *Fine as you are* sounded patronising and just way, way too little, so he settled for 'lovely' instead, which seemed sort of safe and couldn't be construed as flirting, because he wasn't flirting. Well, he didn't think he was.

'And I'm not lazy.'

'I know that!' Angus answered, 'I worked with you yesterday—I know that you're far from lazy!'

'And…' Imogen gave a cheeky grin as he reached for his mug '…Brad was wrong on the final count too!'

'Quite!' He took a gulp of his coffee.

'Just in case you were wondering!' She winked.

He wasn't going to answer that one!

So she tried another question instead. 'Was she

worried, Gemma?' Imogen flushed just a little as she fished. 'About you and the nanny?'

'Ainslie!' Angus shot her an incredulous look.

'Just wondering.' Imogen shrugged. 'Just you said that you went to see her this morning…'

'Because she was thrown out of my house!' He didn't even hide his annoyance at her suggestion. 'Because, like you, she's from Australia, and in the same way I was concerned about you yesterday…' He stopped in mid-sentence, because for the first time in the entire conversation he was veering from the truth. His concern for Ainslie had been as an employer, whereas his concern for Imogen… Angus swallowed hard. 'Look,' he said brusquely, 'I can assure you Gemma wasn't, neither did she have any reason to be, jealous.'

'Then consider me assured!'

'In fact—' Angus bristled with indignation '—it's Gemma who's been having an affair.'

'So things weren't happy at home?'

'You don't know that,' Angus started, but she was right, because the facts spoke for themselves. Eventually he nodded. 'She says she didn't intend to have an affair, but she fell in love.'

'Well, you can't plan for that,' Imogen said.

'You can when you're married.' Angus argued then gave in. 'OK, yes—things weren't good at home. We were both holding on till Clemmie went to school—it was over a long time ago. Gemma's a model,' he explained. 'She stopped working when we had the children, then when Clemmie was one she went back to it. Till that point, even before we had kids, it had been pretty low key, catalogues, brochures that type of thing. Then suddenly things just took off for her in a way neither of us expected really. I supported her at the start, well I hope I did. That's how I got into this blasted celebrity doctor spot— I was at a television studio where she was being interviewed and they needed an expert opinion…'

'Do you like doing it?'

'Sometimes,' Angus said. 'It's certainly a good forum for education—just sometimes…' He gave a tight shrug, not noticing her slight smile at the rather formal description. 'It started to take over and I pulled back. Gemma wanted me to do more of the celebrity stuff and wind things down at the hospital, but for me that wasn't an option. I guess, in the end, we just wanted different things.'

'Like what?' Imogen asked, but Angus didn't answer. 'Like what?' she pushed, but Angus just shook his head.

'I don't know,' he admitted. 'We've got great kids, a great home, we love our work…' He blew out a breath of frustration. 'I don't know.'

'Tell me about it…' Imogen sighed then perked up. 'Except Brad's and my home wasn't actually that great and I wasn't particularly happy at work either, but we did have the great-kid bit!'

'Are you always so open?'

'No!' Imogen grinned. 'But given I'm not going to be here for long, and after yesterday I have no intention of working back down in your emergency room again, I think I can afford to be. You can be too!'

'We agreed last year things weren't working…' He gave a pensive smile. 'That makes it sound like we drew a neat conclusion, but it was the toughest thing we'd ever done. We both decided to stay together till Clemmie was at school.'

'In September?' Imogen checked.

'Yep.' Angus nodded. 'I'd signed up till then with the TV station, knowing that once they were both at school, I was going to give it up anyway and become the primary carer.'

'Not Gemma?'

'She figures she's only got a few years of modelling left—as I pointed out to her, the kids only have one childhood…' He drew in a deep breath then let it out. 'For the kids I could live a year or so in a marriage that was over, just not an unfaithful one. Gemma, it would seem, couldn't. After I got back from speaking with Ainslie this morning, we had an almighty row and the truth came out. Gemma did what I always knew she would in the end…' His eyes were two balls of pain. 'She walked out on the kids.'

'Do they know?'

'They know that she'll be away for a few days. I've told them she's away on a photo shoot, they're pretty used to that… I'm hoping that she'll see sense.'

'That she'll come back?' Imogen checked, but Angus shook his head.

'That we can work out properly what we're going to tell them—*then* tell the kids together. But, no—she's not coming back.'

'So what now?'

'Don't know…' he admitted. 'My mum's in Scotland. I'll ring her tonight, ask her to come and help out for a couple of weeks…'

'Will she be terribly upset?'

'I don't know,' Angus said. 'I'm going to have to ask her though…' He gave a small grimace as he realized how many other busy lives would be disrupted by his. 'She's going to visit friends for a few days for Christmas. I'll ask her to come after that—at least till I find a new nanny. My sister, Lorna, lives nearby. I'm sure she can help out sometimes, although she is working…'

'So you have got a plan!'

'Sort of.'

'Good.'

'Which doesn't help now.' He took another mouthful of coffee then screwed up his face. 'This is cold—do you want another?'

She didn't, but she nodded, and Angus idly watched from the counter as she sat and checked her phone as he ordered a couple of coffees and two mini Christmas puddings, surprised himself at how much better he felt now just by talking.

'Don't you miss Heath?' Angus asked Imogen, though he was still thinking about Gemma. 'When he's with his dad?'

'All the time!' Imogen answered. 'I feel like I've permanently forgotten my keys when he isn't around. I confess to being the world's most overprotective mother— Brad always said he'd turn out to be a mummy's boy if I didn't back off, but he's turned out quite the opposite…'

'So how…' Angus frowned '…can you stand for him to live in London and you in Australia?' This time it was Imogen looking at him as if he'd gone stark raving mad in the middle of the café! 'You said he was here with his dad.'

'He is,' Imogen answered slowly, 'because I brought him here.'

'Oh!'

'Brad doesn't live here!' She smiled at his confusion. 'Brad and I pretty much share care back home in Queensland,' Imogen explained. 'Though, given the nature of his work, it tends to fall on me. When he got offered this role, well, it was huge for him. They've got time off over the Christmas break, but it would have been practically impossible for him to get home and he didn't want to be apart from Heath for Christmas. It's just a one-off—you see, he's got terminal cancer.'

'Oh, my God!'

'Not Brad!' Imogen grinned at his appalled expression. 'His character—Shane. He only took the part because it was short term—just three months. Brad would never come and live here and leave Heath. He's only going to be in England for a few more weeks, but even though I really wanted Heath to have some time in London, and some real quality time with his dad, I just couldn't stand to be away from him over Christmas. So I said that I'd bring him over, but that I'd stay pretty much in the background. I mean, Heath's having a ball, I've just taken him over to the studio now—he's watching his dad and all the cast are spoiling him. I don't want to interrupt that…'

'You're amazing,' Angus said.

'Amazing and broke!' Imogen admitted. 'This little

jaunt to support my ex-husband's rising career has cost an absolute fortune—the airfares, the accommodation, my mad moment on the London Eye—'

'Worth it?' Angus broke in.

'Very much so!' Imogen smiled. 'I took Heath to see Buckingham Palace this morning, which was just amazing. Mind you, I'm already sick of taking him to cafes for lunch. I don't want him staying with me at the youth hostel—but I can't afford to stay anywhere else…' Her voice trailed off as she caught him frowning. Their eyes locked for just a fraction of time, then both rapidly looked away concentrating on their mini Christmas puddings.

'You could always…' Angus broke the sudden silence then blew out a breath, before looking at her again. Serious, practical, yet somehow terribly hazardous, she offered a taste of a solution. 'Look, I'm minus a nanny. The nanny's empty room might not be the best on offer, but I'm sure that it would beat the youth hostel…'

'I don't want to be a nanny.' Imogen gave a polite smile. 'I am trying to have a bit of a holiday, believe it or not.'

'I'm not asking you for that.' Angus cleared his throat. 'Just helping out a friend and you'd be helping me too. It makes sense.'

'Why would you do that?' Imogen asked, and he opened his mouth to respond only Angus couldn't, because if it had been anyone else at work in her predicament, he wasn't sure that he'd make the same offer. In fact, he wouldn't even be having this conversation, would never dream of telling anyone at work so much about him and Gemma. There was just no point of reference—nothing familiar—and not a hope of answering her question.

'It would be bliss to actually have Heath stay over with me for a couple of nights during the week, and that's not going to happen at the youth hostel.' Her voice dragged him out of his introspection. 'I could juggle my shifts around yours... Are you sure about this, Angus?' Imogen asked.

'Absolutely.' Angus answered, without thinking, but when his brain caught up the conclusion was the same. 'Absolutely.'

'Just till your mum gets here?'

'Whatever suits you.'

'How soon...?'

'When can I...?'

They both laughed as they spoke over each other.

'Why don't I go home and speak to the kids?' Angus suggested. 'You go and pack up your stuff. Then, if it's OK, I'll dash over to the hospital and tell them....'

'Tell them what?'

'That I...' He opened his mouth, closed it, then opened it again. 'I'm on all day tomorrow... Are you sure?'

'Works perfectly for me!' Imogen answered. 'I'm on a day off.'

CHAPTER SIX

PACKING up her things at the youth hostel didn't take Imogen long. Angus had assured her his house was easy to find and was a mere two minutes' walk from an underground station. She had his address and phone number in her pocket, but as Imogen sat on the tube, her heart was hammering.

It had all made perfect sense at the time.

Sitting in the café with him, talking to him, confident and relaxed in his company, it had seemed an obvious solution for both of them. The last night at the hostel had been hell—the noise, the laughter, the sheer energy of the place just too much to deal with, when all she'd wanted was to flop in front of the television and *not* think about her day. It was also no place to bring Heath and although she was desperate to cram in as much sightseeing as possible with him, she was already tired of sitting in cafés with him. A homebody by anyone's standards, at the end of the day Imogen wanted to be in rather than out, wanted to just be with her son rather than think up things to amuse him.

It just didn't make perfect sense now.

Coming out from the underground station and finding Angus's street easily, Imogen was tempted to turn and run in the other direction as she wheeled her suitcase towards yet another destination unknown.

And how she hated them.

Hated the chaos her life had been plunged into when Heath had been just a baby. She had spent the last three years extricating herself from it.

Sensible might just as well be her middle name. She never took risks, never did things on impulse, well, hadn't done in a long time. As *amazing* as Angus thought she was for coming to London, he hadn't known the angst it had caused her to be hurtled out of the comfort zone she had created for herself and Heath back home in Australia. He wouldn't have a clue how out of character it was for her to have asked him for coffee, to sit in a café with a man she'd only just met and *then* agree to move in with him!

And he couldn't possibly have known how much courage it took for her to knock on his door and smile widely as he opened it.

'This is Imogen…' Angus introduced her as he led her through to the lounge. 'She's a nurse from the hospital and she's going to help out for a little while.'

'Will Ainslie come back?' Clemmie, her hair thick with curls and her eyes as green as Angus's, gave Imogen a bored glance then spoke to her father.

'No, Ainslie's got a job with a new family now,' Angus answered.

'Ainslie was fun!' Dark eyed and dark haired, Jack looked directly at Imogen as he threw down a challenge.

'I can manage fun.' Imogen smiled, unfazed. 'I like your Christmas tree!'

Actually, she didn't. On the positive side, at least it was a *real* Christmas tree, but it was so tastefully decorated it surely belonged in a department store. Large silver ribbons and not a lot else dressed the lonely branches, and several, beautifully wrapped silver boxes lay strategically underneath, causing the children to stand to rigid attention when Imogen strolled over and picked one up.

'You're not supposed to touch!' Clemmie warned.

'Whoops! Are they for display purposes only?' Imogen smiled, replacing the empty box.

'I made a decoration at school…' Jack scampered out and returned with several pieces of pasta stuck on a card and sprayed gold.

'That's fabulous!' Imogen beamed, placing it on the tree and standing back to admire it. 'Maybe we can make some more tomorrow when your dad's at work—if that's OK with you guys!'

'Imogen is *not* the new nanny,' Angus warned his children. 'She's a friend, helping out for now, so remember that.

'Come on.' He smiled. 'I'll show you around.'

The children didn't follow, and now, back in his company, chatting easily as he showed her around his home, it all made perfect sense again. Even though it was an enigma to Imogen, from the two busy schedules that were pinned up on the fridge the Maitlin family was obviously used to having staff, used to having people living in their home, cleaning their things *and* looking after their children.

'The children have a separate menu?' Imogen frowned as she looked at a piece of paper attached to the fridge.

'I'm not expecting you to follow it.' Angus laughed. 'That was for Ainslie. Anyway, the children have already had tea…' Which did nothing to fade her frown. 'At my sister's.'

'You mean dinner?'

Still, apart from the endless lists, the house was gorgeous.

Well, apart from the endless photos.

For the most part she was comfortable with her body. Sure, Brad's words had hurt at the time and for a good while after that, but, as her mother had pointed out, her whole family might be curvy, big bosomed and big bottomed, but they weren't unhealthy. Imogen's sister had also pointed out, furiously jabbing at a magazine to reiterate the point, that no woman who had had children could possibly, without a lot of airbrushing, look like that!

'When was that taken?' Imogen paused at a particularly spectacular image of a woman rising from the ocean in a man's white shirt.

'The year before last…' Angus frowned. 'When we went to Thailand, supposedly to try and make things work.'

'It's lovely,' Imogen said, deciding to take a photo of her own to send as a postcard to her sister!

Used to airy, open-plan houses, painted walls and floorboards, Imogen adored the old house. The carpets were thick and cream and the bold choices of colour on the wallpapered walls were so different to their own house—even the stairs would be a novelty for Heath.

She could practically see him surfing his way down them head first. There was even a little box bedroom, which at first Imogen assumed was for her but was actually a spare that, Angus told her, she was welcome to use for Heath.

'This is yours.' He led her up yet another set of stairs to the 'nanny's accommodation', which translated to a converted attic decorated in white and yellow, with a skylight that had blinds and even a little kitchenette with a microwave, fridge and kettle.

'Does anyone actually eat together in this house?'

'I don't expect you to hide away in the attic,' Angus said. 'There's no bathroom facilities up here, though…'

'I wasn't expecting there to be.'

'Getting and keeping a good nanny is a serious business here,' Angus explained to a thoroughly bemused Imogen. 'Ideally they should have their own self-contained accommodation.'

'So you don't have to see them!'

'It's the other way around.' Angus laughed. 'They don't want to see us on their time off. Honestly, it's like a minefield.'

And one she had no intention of walking through!

Especially when at seven p.m., Clemmie informed Imogen that she'd forgotten to put her pyjamas out on her bed for her.

'Ainslie always did!' Clemmie said tearfully when Angus scolded her.

'Imogen is not the new nanny. I've told you she's a friend who's helping us out. Imogen's got a job at the hospital and her own little boy to look after.'

'How old is he?' Clemmie asked, suddenly interested.

'Four—like you. He's called Heath.'

'Well, my dad's on the television!' Clemmie said proudly.

'So's Heath's dad!' Imogen said, equally as proudly, then glanced at her watch. 'May I?'

'Help yourself,' Angus answered, somewhat bemused as the three of them piled on the sofa and proceeded to watch what was surely unsuitable viewing for a four- and a five-year-old, but from the squeals of recognition it wasn't the first time they had seen the show and from their rapt expressions it wouldn't be the last.

'Shane's Heath's dad?' Jack checked, clearly impressed.

'Cool!' Clemmie chanted.

And when surely he should be frantic, should be ringing round relatives, thinking about lawyers, trying to contact Gemma, for the moment at least he paused.

'Ten minutes,' Angus warned the children, 'then it's time to get ready for bed.'

Not that they were listening, all eyes in the room drawn to six feet two of bronzed Australian muscle, Shane's sun-bleached blond hair long and tousled on the pillow of his hospital bed. As if on cue Imogen's mobile began to ring.

'Hey, Brad!' Absolutely at ease, she grinned into the phone. 'I'm watching you now—tell them to go easy on the blusher next time…' Then she spoke with her son and Angus wondered if he and Gemma could ever get there, could chat and grin and even manage a laugh. Right now that world seemed light years away. Later, when Clemmie and Jack were in bed, and Imogen was rather expertly pulling a cork out of a bottle of her duty-free wine, Angus thought that perhaps now was the time he should be overcome with emotion, grief, panic, when *surely* now he should be thinking about tracking down his errant wife, or ringing his family, or getting started the million and one tasks that surely lay ahead. Instead, he pulled two steaks out of the freezer and watched as their dinner defrosted through the glass door of the microwave, watched as Imogen chopped onions and mushrooms and added a dash of wine to the sauce for the steaks, and it seemed incongruous how good he actually felt.

'To you!' Imogen tapped his glass and took a sip. 'To getting through.'

'I don't know how I would have, especially with it being Christmas…'

'You would have.'

'I would,' he agreed, taking another sip, 'but it would have messed up a lot of people's plans. This is really nice wine, by the way.'

'We do a good red.' Imogen smiled. 'I've got five more bottles upstairs!' Then she was serious. 'The kids seem OK.'

'They're used to people coming and going, and they're used to Gemma being away. They seem more upset that Ainslie's gone at the moment… though they'll be devastated when I tell them about their mother and me.'

'Just wait till Gemma's calmed down,' Imogen said wisely. 'Things might look different.'

'We won't be getting back together.' The slight raise of her brows irritated him. 'Once I've made up my mind, Imogen, I don't change it.'

It was a nice dinner—a *really* nice dinner—just talking about work, and about Angus trying to cram in an eighty-hour working week at the hospital and also look after a family. They talked about Imogen's life in Australia and her colossal mortgage, how she missed midwifery and how she juggled her shifts around Heath and Brad and she told him how much easier things would be in a few weeks once Heath started school.

'Are you seeing anyone?'

Oh, so casually he said it—well, she knew so much about him, surely it was right to ask?

'No.' She frowned over her wineglass at him. 'You?'

'I've only been separated for…' he glanced at his watch '…oh, ten hours now.'

That wasn't what she'd been asking, but from the way he'd answered she didn't need to clarify the question. Somehow Imogen knew that the man sitting at the table, leaning over to top up her glass, was as decent and as nice as he appeared.

As he went to fill her glass, both shared a quick yikes look when they realised the bottle was empty.

'I'm going to bed.' Imogen stretched as she stood.

'It's not even nine o'clock.'

'Perhaps, but I'm still jet-lagged.'

'Sorry—I keep forgetting you've only just got here. You just seem so….' His voice trailed off, not sure himself what he had been trying to say. ''Night, Imogen, and thanks, thanks for all your help today.'

''Night, Angus.'

Familiar.

As he stacked the dishwasher Angus shook his head, unhappy with the description.

Comfortable.

Only that didn't fit either, because at every turn she shocked him, shocked himself too—he'd told her things he never thought he'd share.

She'd been right about so many things, though, Angus thought, and it had been good to talk, to be honest, to share some of what he was going through.

Though there was one thing that she'd got wrong...

Picking up the phone, he rang his mother, took a deep breath and paused for the longest time when she answered the phone.

'Is anybody there?'

'It's me, Angus.'

Yes, Imogen was wrong, because his marriage to Gemma really was over. Angus knew that for sure, or he'd never have made that call.

Imogen stared at the ceiling as she listened to the low murmur of Angus's voice drifting up the stairs as he spoke on the telephone. Suddenly she found she was holding her breath too.

In three years she'd barely even glanced at another man—let alone flirt.

Oh, and she had been flirting. Not deliberately—in fact, only now, lying in bed and going over the day, was

Imogen blushing as red as her hair as she recalled some of the things that she'd said. They'd been the sort of cheeky, flirty things the old Imogen would have said a million years ago when she and Brad had been happy.

What *had* she been thinking? Imogen scolded herself.

Angus Maitlin was married to a model, for heaven's sake, or had *just* broken up with her. As if he'd even *think* of her in that way. And he was only being nice because he was glad she was here, that was all. Without her, a lot of people's Christmas plans would have been messed up and he would have had to fly his mother down from Scotland or try and arrange rapid child care just a week before Christmas. Yes, he was just glad she was here.

She was glad she was here too!

Everyone had said she was crazy, zipping over to London when she could least afford it, and had told her that she was being too soft on Brad, that he was taking advantage of her, but it was actually the other way around.

She needed this, Imogen thought. Lying in a strange bed, in a strange house, in a strange country, in the middle of an English winter—she actually felt as if she was thawing out.

As if the Imogen that had been placed in cold storage when her marriage had broken down and she had struggled just to survive was making itself known again.

So what if she had been flirting? She was testing her wings, that was all.

As the phone pinged off, as the rumble of pipes through the house stilled, as she heard the heavy creak of the stairs, never had a house been more noisy, but as quiet filled her little attic Imogen stared up at the skylight, too tired to close the blinds now, a streetlight outside illuminating low clouds as they drifted past, the sky lighter than it had been at nine that morning, which didn't make sense, but she was too tired to work it out.

Yes, she needed this, Imogen realised, turning on her side and letting delicious waves of sleep wash over her.

Needed to be where no one actually knew her, so that maybe, just maybe she could find herself again.

CHAPTER SEVEN

AN EYEFUL of grey and the thick sound of nothing woke her up.

Staring at the skylight, struggling to orientate herself, the snowflakes falling was nothing like she'd dreamed of. The wad of grey slush peeled away from the edge of the skylight and slid down the glass and as Imogen climbed out of bed she found out for the first time what it *really* meant to be cold. She was tempted to tell Angus why he couldn't keep a nanny!

'Sorry!' Grinning, just back from a run, Angus looked as warm as the toast he was buttering. 'The heating timer's not working. I meant to put it on before my run. The house will warm up soon.'

'You run in snow!'

'It's not snowing!' Angus refuted. 'Though it is trying to. It's turning to slush as soon as it hits the ground.'

Handing her a cup of tea, Imogen wasn't sure if it was her breath or the steam that was coming out of her mouth. Disgustingly healthy, brimming with energy, Angus joined her, but she started to forgive him when he proceeded to spread thick marmalade on a mountain of toast. He *did* have nice hands, large yet neat, with short white nails and a flash of an expensive watch. Imogen noticed his left hand was now minus a wedding ring.

'Did you want marmalade?' He checked when he caught her looking.

'Thanks!' Imogen said, and forgave him completely when he didn't moan that she ate more than half of the toast.

'Any plans for today?'

'None as yet…' The whole day stretched out before her—three kids and the whole of London waiting to be explored, and she'd take her time deciding. 'I want to do the Duck Tour…' She misread his frown. 'I saw it on the Internet—this bus takes you around London then straight onto the river.'

'I know what it is —are you really going to do that?'

'Maybe…' Imogen shrugged. 'Or I might wait for a warmer day.'

It irked her that he laughed.

Imogen Von Trapp she was not, but with accommodation sorted, and her three little charges marching beside her with maps in hand, Imogen felt close. She snapped away with her camera as Heath, Clemmie and Jack teased the solider at the Horse Guard Parade—Clemmie furious she couldn't extract a smile. There was so much to see, and while she was here Imogen fully intended to see it all, but by mid-afternoon her charges were sagging. Cracking a bar of chocolate on the tube, she tried to inject some enthusiasm as they headed for Knightsbridge.

'I don't want to go shopping!' Heath moaned.

'Not even if you get to see Santa?' Imogen checked.

'It's not the real one!' Jack scolded. 'Everyone knows that they just send a helper to the shops!'

'Oh, no!' Imogen cajoled. 'Everyone knows that the *real* Santa only goes to Harrods!'

Every time he saw her she was more beautiful.

As if the first image of her had been in black and white, and not so gradually the colour was being turned up. She was wearing her black skirt and flat boots again only with fishnet stockings this time and a sort of dusky pink jumper that was clearly too warm for her in the kitchen, because there was a pink glow to her cheeks. He noticed this because she was wearing long silver earrings that caught the light as she smiled up at him from the table where she was sitting.

'Angus, this is Brad.' Imogen introduced them as Angus walked in the kitchen after an extremely long day.

'Hi, there!' Blond, long limbed and utterly at ease, Brad grinned up at him from the kitchen table, where they sat with two mugs of tea. Then Brad looked at Imogen, saw the tint that spread up to her cheeks, saw the slight flurry of her hands, the rapid way she blinked when she was suddenly nervous—and knew it was time to go.

'Hello!' Angus said politely, pulling out a chair and joining them, only his heart wasn't in it. There was this niggling pain in his stomach now, causing him to wonder if the stress might be catching up with him and he was getting an ulcer.

'And this…' Imogen said as six little feet charged down the stairs and into the kitchen, skidding to a halt, 'is Heath.'

'Hi!' Bold, confident and a mini-version of his father, Heath grinned up at him, showing a spectacular gap where his baby teeth had once been.

'Hi, there!'

Clemmie was dancing on the spot and thrusting a photo at him, 'Imogen took us to see Santa!'

'It's not the fake one!' Jack warned. 'Imogen took us to see the real one.'

'Fantastic!' Angus duly said, only it was a great photo—three beaming faces and one very flustered-looking Santa. Suddenly Angus was grinning too, 'Wow!' he added. 'You really did meet the real thing.'

'The food hall was fabulous too!' Imogen said, heading to the kettle to make Angus a drink. 'I thought I'd died and gone to heaven. I'm worn out now, though!'

'I'd better get going.' Brad smiled as the kids all scampered off to the lounge.

'Don't rush off on my account!' Angus offered, but Brad was already on his way out, standing at the kitchen door and calling for Heath to hurry up and say goodbye.

'Think about what I said, Imo,' Brad added as he waited. 'It might be nice for Heath to wake up on Christmas morning with us both there.'

'It would be too confusing for him,' Imogen called. 'I'll come over about ten.'

And even though Brad's voice was laid-back and casual, as Angus watched Brad watching Imogen, he knew he was anything but. Knew, that the, oh, so laid-back Brad, still fancied his ex-wife.

'Think about it!' Brad said, again calling for Heath and getting the little guy into his coat, then giving Imogen a bit more than a friendly kiss on the cheek. He ought to think about eating, Angus decided, because his stomach was really starting to hurt now.

'Come and see the tree!' Clemmie declared, once Brad and Heath had gone. 'Santa gave us glitter-glue and paper…'

'Oh, my!' Angus whistled through his teeth as he walked into the lounge. The once tastefully decorated tree was now a blaze of multicoloured stars and angels and some other shapes he couldn't quite decipher. 'It's brilliant!' Angus declared to the kids, and then added under his breath for Imogen's benefit, 'Gemma will have a coronary!'

'I did think about that!' Imogen admitted, 'but when Santa gives you glue and glitter pens and there's a tree just begging for colour…'

'You've got glitter in your hair.'

'I've got glitter *everywhere*!' Imogen responded, pushing the arms up on her V-neck jumper and revealing some glittery forearms. 'I'll never get it off!'

'You and Brad are friendly,' Angus commented a little while later, frying up chicken that was generously dressed with tarragon, while Imogen made a vast salad.

'We are now!' Imogen answered, pulling a mango out of the fridge.

'Where the hell did you get that?'

'The food hall at Harrods,' Imogen laughed, 'I told you it was fabulous. I just couldn't resist—it reminded me of home.'

'So, you're just friends now?' Angus prolonged the conversation, not the one about the fruit, which she was expertly slicing, instead broaching the other things that reminded her of home.

'Brad's a great guy and he's a wonderful dad...' Imogen shrugged. 'He's just a lousy husband!' She poured the hot chicken and oil over the cold salad, added the mango and tossed it all in together as the four of them sat down to eat.

'What's this?' Jack, who did his level best not to eat anything green, let alone salad in December, frowned at his dinner.

'Imogen's warm chicken salad,' Imogen announced, as if she'd lifted the recipe from a book. 'And it's bliss!'

It was, just the thing his grumbling ulcer needed, Angus decided, slicing a crusty bread stick, stunned again at the normality of it all, or rather the abnormality of it all, as for the second time in as many days he sat down to a nice home-cooked dinner.

'The agency rang, they asked if I could do a late shift tomorrow.' Imogen took a big gulp of water. 'I said I'd get back to them, but I just saw your roster on the fridge and it's got "OC" written over tomorrow—am I right in assuming that's "on call"?'

'It just changed to "OAN"—or "on all night".' Angus grinned. 'Gus has a do to go to, but it's not a problem— I've already rung Lorna and she's going to have the kids tomorrow night, so take the shift.'

'You're sure?' Imogen checked. 'I can always ring the agency.'

'No need.' Angus said, helping himself to seconds. As easily as that it was sorted, no histrionics, no 'What about *my* career?'—just a simple solution to a simple problem, and for the first time in the longest time Angus actually felt as if he could breathe!

Until she stood up and leant over to load Jack's already empty plate with some more of the nicest warm salad imaginable on a cold December night and treated him to a glimpse of two very freckly, very glittery breasts.

'It gets everywhere, I tell you!' Imogen laughed as she caught him looking then blushed and looked away. 'I'm never going to get it off.'

Later, with the kids in their pyjamas, and the living room beginning to look a lot like Christmas, with the four of them watching Shane kissing a nubile blonde under the mistletoe, Imogen shot him a look.

'Are you OK?'

'Not sure…' Angus said, uncomfortably massaging his stomach. 'You know, I think I might be getting an ulcer.'

'Stress!' Imogen said, turning her head back to the television. 'Have a glass of milk.'

'How many times do I have to say it?' Angus responded, only she wasn't listening. 'I'm fine!'

'I've never seen so many Colles' fractures!'

'It's par for the course on this side of the world.' Heather grinned, as Imogen massaged her aching back.

After Maria, Imogen had never intended to go back to

Emergency, but the agency had rung a few times, and comparing Heath's 'to-do' list in London alongside her bank account, a full late shift, even if it was in Emergency, was one Imogen couldn't really justify declining.

Thankfully it had proven far less eventful that her first shift in London. Oh, it had been busy, but dramas had been few and far between and heading towards her supper break, Imogen had just one more wrist to help plaster.

Colles' fractures often occurred when people put out their hands to save themselves from a fall, and the slushy, icy streets had meant that Imogen had seen more in one shift than she usually would in a year in Queensland. She was happily explaining this to Ivy Banford as she held up her hand while Owen Richards, the intern, plastered it.

'Well, I still feel like an old fool!' Ivy scolded herself. 'As if I'm not enough trouble to everybody already.'

'Trouble?' Imogen frowned, taking in the neatly done-up blouse and smart shoes, the powdered nose and the lips that still held a smudge of coral. 'Since when were you any trouble to anyone?'

Ivy Banford wouldn't know *how* to make trouble. She'd been sitting patiently in the waiting room since eleven a.m., called for an x-Ray at three, and only now, as the clock edged past seven, was her wrist finally having a cast applied. And all she had done was apologise.

'I'm supposed to be at my son William's for Christmas. I wanted to have it at mine, but they all insisted…told me I should relax and let them do it. Now all I'm going to do is get in the way.'

'So there will be no stuffing the turkey?' Imogen

smiled. 'No laying the table or peeling a mountain of potatoes…'

'I said I'd get the parsnips,' Ivy fretted, pointing to her shopping trolley, 'and I said that I'd do the stuffing—'

'Ivy,' Imogen interrupted, 'I'm sure your son's wife is dying to impress you with her Christmas dinner.'

'She just wants to show me she can do it better.' Ivy pouted. 'She fancies herself as a gourmet chef—she's been waiting to get her hands on that turkey for years…'

'Give the baby her bottle!' Imogen said, her smile widening when she realised Angus had come into the plaster room.

'Meaning?'

'Let her do it all,' Imogen explained. 'Your job is to sit there with a big glass of sherry, play with the grandkids and let everyone spoil you for once. And,' Imogen added, 'even if the parsnips are burnt and the turkey's pink, you're to tell her it was the best Christmas dinner ever!'

'I will not,' Ivy thundered. 'What would that achieve?'

'Could be the start of world peace!' Imogen was holding her back now, grateful when Angus came and took the heavy arm from her as Owen continued to work on Ivy's wrist. 'Try it!'

'Huh!' Ivy huffed, but a small smile was forming. 'She'd get the shock of her life, mind!'

'And she'd know you didn't mean it!' Owen chimed in, as Imogen popped Ivy's arm into a sling.

'Just because you act like a sweet old thing…' Imogen winked '…doesn't mean you are one!'

'Your relatives are here,' Heather said as she ushered in a worried-looking man followed by his grim-faced wife.

'Oh, Mum, what have you been doing?'

'I'm fine, William!' Ivy said, refusing his help with her coat. Catching Imogen's eye, she relented and let him help her put it on. 'I didn't manage to get the parsnips.'

'Doesn't matter a scrap, Mum!' William soothed. 'Elise has got everything under control.'

'Such a relief…' Ivy smiled warmly at her daughter-in-law. 'I've a feeling this is going to be the best Christmas yet. Elise, dear, would you pass me my purse?'

But even before she'd pried out a note with one hand, Imogen was on to her.

'Don't you dare, Ivy!'

'Buy some sweets for your little boy!' Ivy insisted, pressing the note into Imogen's hand.

'I'll buy his sweets!' Imogen stuffed the fiver back in the purse and snapped it closed. 'You put it towards your sherry!'

'You're incorrigible.' Owen grinned as the trio shuffled off.

'I'm thirsty too!' Imogen smiled. 'I'm going for my break.'

'Good idea!' Owen agreed, following her out and telling Heather he'd be back in fifteen minutes. The sound of their laughter drifted down the corridor and Angus felt a kick in his stomach again.

'Everything OK?' Heather checked, as she noticed Angus rubbing his abdomen.

'Everything's fine!' Angus nodded then changed his mind, 'Actually, Heather, you couldn't get me some Gaviscon or Mylanta…?'

'For who? Did I miss someone?'

'It's actually for me.' Angus pulled a face. 'I think I've got an ulcer. I'm going to get some milk.'

It was a quiet evening—'The lull before the storm,' Heather warned, pouring out a dose of antacid then handing it to Angus. 'Better?' Heather checked, as Angus downed the chalky brew.

'Thanks.'

But walking into the staffroom, to find Imogen and Owen giggling as *Celebrity Doctor* calmly discussed some rather intimate issues, didn't exactly help.

'Do we have to watch this?' Angus snapped. 'It's actually a serious subject if you bothered to listen.'

'Sorry!' Imogen smothered a smile and though clearly not remotely sorry she did change the channel. However, this meant that he had to sit and watch a certain blonde head, *again*, writhing on the pillow, only this time in pain as the doctors battled to save Shane.

'He's gorgeous!' Another nurse, Cassie, had joined them now, gaping at the screen then over at Imogen, clearly unable to comprehend that someone as gorgeous as *Shane* could ever have married someone as plain and as overweight as Imogen. 'And he's such a good actor.'

'Do you think so?' Imogen sounded surprised. 'He's a complete hypochondriac. He carried on exactly like that when he had toothache.'

The storm didn't eventuate. The lull stretched on and when the night staff started to arrive, Heather had sent most of her regular staff home, knowing the night shift would dash around if there was an emergency. A few nurses milled around what patients there were and

Imogen filled in the time by doing a restock as Heather and Angus chatted.

'Ready for Christmas?' Heather asked Angus as she updated the whiteboard.

'Hope so.'

'Don't worry—I'm sure Gemma's got it all under control.'

'Actually, Heather…Gemma and I broke up.' Imogen watched as Heather's hand paused over the whiteboard, her face aghast as she turned around. 'It's fine, Heather.'

'It's not fine!' Heather looked as if she was about to cry. 'Angus, why didn't you say?'

'I just did.'

'But…'

'Look!' Angus gave a wry smile. 'I'm just letting you know in case something unforseen happens—Gus has offered to help out if need be.'

'So where are the kids?'

'At home.'

'Where's Gemma?' As Angus gave a small eye roll, Heather sagged. 'When did all this happen? Oh, Angus…'

'It's all under control.'

'But how?' Heather asked. 'Who's helping with the kids?'

Imogen swallowed hard, her cheeks darkening a touch, wondering if Angus would say anything, and how Heather would react if he did. There was no need to worry, Angus's next comment making it spectacularly clear that his home and work lives were kept very separate.

'I've got some temporary help for now and my mother is coming down to stay after Christmas.'

He smiled over at Imogen, only she didn't smile back. In fact, she looked away.

Temporary.

Strange how much that word had stung her to hear.

Temporary.

Funny that the same word buzzed like a blowfly around Angus for the rest of his night shift.

And when she said goodnight, when the quiet department suddenly seemed empty without her, when he joined Owen later in the staffroom and had to listen to his junior tell him how great that red-headed agency nurse was, two weeks suddenly seemed too short.

His marriage was over, his life was supposed to be in chaos, Christmas was just a couple of days away and yet he was coping, would make sure that the kids coped, knew that they'd all get through.

The only thing that daunted him at this moment was the prospect of Imogen leaving.

That temporary solution he had found raised an entirely new set of problems all of a sudden.

CHAPTER EIGHT

ON SHEER impulse Imogen had purchased a red bikini and sheer silver sarong at the departure terminal in Queensland.

She'd had absolutely no intention of wearing them until she got home, and they'd nestled in her case with the labels still on. But, waking at the crack of dawn, her sleeping pattern still horribly out of whack, finally she had a reason to put them on.

Angus had point blank refused to take rent.

Admittedly she hadn't pushed the point, but the bliss of having a nice roof over her head for her time in London and as much work as she wanted meant Imogen could pay him back in other ways—like mangos—and at 5.30 a.m., when restless legs started twitching, she decided she could give the bathroom a rather overdue clean, because Mrs Gemma Maitlin certainly hadn't picked up the cleaning baton when she'd fired the cleaning lady!

Wrinkling up her nose, Imogen peered into the shower. Housework wasn't exactly her forte, but occasionally the urge hit, and it was hitting now. Turning up the heating and grabbing the radio as she located the cleaning gear, she padded to the bathroom, dropping her sarong in the hallway and frowning at her reflection in the bathroom mirror.

'Diet!' she warned herself, turning round and grimacing at her bottom, but at least it was tanned—brown fat was certainly more attractive than white! Yes, in the new year she was definitely going on diet.

'But after we get back!' she promised her reflection. Then she promptly forgot about it as she bopped along to the music, glad by the time that she'd finished and jet-lag had hit that Angus's kids were at his sister's and Heath was with Brad, so that she could now head down to the kitchen, grab a cup of tea and crawl back into bed before Angus came home.

Then she heard his key in the front door.

Eyes wide, her face red from exertion, Imogen wondered what she should do. She could just stand in the bathroom and hope he didn't notice or she could make a dash to her room. But if he looked up he'd see her running across the landing and she could hear his foot on the bottom step now so, not wanting to stink of bleach, she sprayed a generous dash of perfume and forced a smile on her face as she headed out to meet him.

Tired, grumpy and freezing, all Angus wanted to do as he put the key in the front door and headed up the stairs was to fall into bed.

Tired, because he'd been up all night.

Grumpy, because his shirt, suit and tie had lasted till seven a.m. but were now in a plastic bag, awaiting a trip to the dry cleaner's. Tossing the bag in the corner, he decided to deal with that unpleasant task later.

Freezing, because hair wet from a quick shower at work and dressed now in threadbare theatre gear, he'd found out five minutes from home that he really should have stopped for petrol at the last garage.

The heat hit him as soon as he stepped into the hall—the place was like a sauna!

He didn't have the energy to work out why—all he wanted was bed.

Till he saw Imogen standing on the landing.

'Morning!'

'Morning!' Angus gave what he hoped was a normal smile as he stood at the bottom of the stairs, trying not to look surprised or to comment on the fact that she was wearing nothing other than a red bikini. He failed miserably on both counts. 'Imogen!' He gaped. 'Why are you dressed like that?'

'I was just cleaning the shower…'

'You wear a bikini to clean the shower?'

'No!' She gave him a very old-fashioned look. 'Normally I wear *nothing* to clean the showers, but given this is your home…'

Picking up a sliver of silver fabric from the floor, she wrapped it around her rather magnificent bosom. 'Do you want some breakfast?'

'Nope!' Funny that he had to feign a yawn now. 'I'm going straight to bed, I want to grab a few hours before I pick up the kids.'

'I'll pick up the kids,' Imogen offered. 'You should have something to eat and then you'll sleep well.'

He'd sleep well without something to eat, Angus was about to say, but she was walking down the stairs and was passing him now, and it would seem rude just to head on up. So Angus followed her into the kitchen, yawning again, but for real this time, as he sat on a barstool and poured some muesli into a bowl as Imogen screwed up her nose.

'I'll make you some pancakes.'

'Muesli's fine.'

'Not after a night shift!' Imogen said, tipping the lot into the bin and, Angus realised, refusing to look at him. 'It will only take a moment.'

'Great,' Angus said.

'There's some mango left…' She pulled it from the fridge, holding up half a fruit, and without waiting for his reply ran the knife along the plump fruit, scoring it into little crosses, then pushing her fingers onto the soft skin and inverting it so that all the fruit poked up into little squares and it felt strangely erotic.

She probably walked around like this at home all the time, Angus frantically reasoned. Wandering around the house in a bikini was probably the norm where she came from. Only there were kangaroos in Australia too, but he didn't expect to see one when he looked out of the window. Still, Angus told himself, she no doubt spent her entire day wearing as little as possible—only that thought wasn't exactly helping matters either!

The huge kitchen was claustrophobically tiny now, and he could see her freckly breasts jiggling before his eyes as she whipped up the batter.

'Won't be long!' Imogen smiled.

'The heating's high…' Angus said gruffly.

'Is it?' Imogen shrugged.

He could hear the batter sizzling as it hit the frying pan. Her back was to him and it was brown, this gorgeous brown that was so rare these days. Her tan not perfect because he could see the straps where another bikini must have been, could see the freckles that showered her back, only it looked pretty perfect to him…

'Here.' Leaning over the bench, she handed him breakfast and as she leant forward he could see the white of her breast as her bikini shifted, saw a little bit of Imogen that had never seen the sun. He knew she'd caught him looking because she was looking at him too, knew because the already hot room was stifling now. The bubbling steam from the kettle nothing compared to the cauldron sizzling between them. Three days after one's marriage ended was arguably the best or worst time to act on impulse—only Angus wasn't actually thinking about that.

For ages his marriage had been over and there was this assumption, from his mother, from Gemma, even from Imogen at first, that he must, in that time, have been seeing someone else. As if coping with the demise and subsequent end of his marriage couldn't have been enough to keep him occupied. Oh, they hadn't come right out and said it, but he could sense they thought there had to be more.

Well, there hadn't been anyone.

But, yes, there was more.

Pushing a plate towards him, loaded with pancakes and mango and syrup, Angus's mouth should have been watering, only it was a touch dry as he realised that there was way more to it than anyone knew.

And he was looking right at her.

Only now Imogen wasn't looking away, as she always had before. In fact, she was looking right at him. For the first time in the longest time, the first time for ages, the woman Angus wanted was looking back at him…

And with want in her eyes.

He *was* beautiful.

She'd known that from the start.

And he was nice.

She'd known that too.

But that this august yet tender man might actually want her in the way she wanted him was, for Imogen, a revelation.

Embarrassed at being caught in her bikini, she'd attempted casual—had, oh, so casually covered herself with her sarong and wished, as she often did, that she'd kept to her diet, or even considered that he might come home early. There were so many things Imogen hadn't factored in, and seeing the want in his eyes as she'd come down the stairs had been one of them.

Oh, she'd dismissed it, told herself she was imagining things.

But, standing in the kitchen, attempting to be normal, she could hear the fizz of arousal sizzling around them. She tried to tell herself over and over that she was misreading things, that it was her want that she could sense and not his.

Only it was everywhere.

She could feel his eyes on her, burning into her back as she turned away, could feel his need in the stifling air she dragged into her tight chest. Awareness in every jerky movement, she was scared to turn around, scared that he might see the tumble of emotions that were coursing through her.

Because, as the kettle rattled to the boil, as she slid the plate she'd prepared towards him, Imogen knew it was impossible, knew that Angus Maitlin could have any woman he wanted...

Only he wanted her.

Watching him stride towards her, she could taste him almost before he kissed her. His mouth on hers had been the last thing she'd expected on awakening, yet it was everything she needed now. Angus made her feel like a woman again, one who had come alive.

For Angus it was the easiest walk of his life.

Used to making difficult decisions in an instant, this one was actually incredibly easy. Oh, he'd wrestled with it for days, had gone over every argument in his head as to why it would never happen, why it could never work, had told himself that he was imagining things, that this vibrant stunning woman saw him as nothing more than a colleague and a friend...

Till she looked up and he saw the pink flush that was ever present in her cheeks spread across her neck and down her chest. He registered the tiny swallow in her throat, and for Angus, walking round the bench and over to her came as naturally as breathing—in fact, more naturally, because breathing was proving difficult right now, his lungs taut. His hands rested on the tops of her arms and he felt her tremulous body beneath them, a body that didn't want soothing, her skin soft and smooth beneath his fingers. He noticed a bergamot note to her perfume as his face neared hers, and it would have been so easy to kiss her then, but haste would have deprived him of seeing those pale blue eyes, black now with pupils dilated with lust. The scent of her skin filled his nostrils and the arousal between them intensified as the feel of her soft cheek grazed against his. He wanted to taste her mouth now so he did, placing his lips on hers and closing his eyes at the exquisite sweetness of ripe flesh that wanted to taste him too—and taste him she did, sucking on his bottom lip. Her hands on his shoulders, fingers kneading lightly as thoroughly he kissed her back.

'Oh, God, Imogen…' He moaned her name as he pulled back, knowing that at this point it should stop, should merit discussion, acknowledgement, something…but the bliss of wanting was here and now and the bliss of being wanted was mind-blowing. She kissed him back, her response moist, lingering, slow, like a river inevitably rolling. He could feel her hands slipping under his theatre top, inquisitive fingers exploring his stomach. He didn't want it to end, wanted also to explore this woman who wore a bikini and sarong on a freezing December morning—who had brought sunshine and warmth into what should have been the bleakest and coldest of winters. His hands, without guidance, were undoing the knot of her sarong, watching two red triangles strain against the gorgeous flesh of her breasts. He wanted to taste the woman who fed him fruit when he wanted bed, and pushing aside the bikini top he lowered his mouth. Her nipples were as hard as hazelnuts swelling in his mouth as he tasted her, his hand on her skin, her back, her waist, feeling the delicious, unfamiliar curves, the generous flesh that was for him, tasting the feel of want on his mouth, these myriad sensations as she kissed him back. And it felt so right—he'd come home this morning and it felt as if he were coming home to her now, to a kiss that had been waiting patiently, to a kiss that was almost *familiar*, because he'd been there before.

He may have said goodnight to her from the day she'd moved in, but he'd met her only a couple of hours later in his dreams. And dreams didn't match up to the real feel of her mouth on his, sucking him, kissing him, devouring him. Imogen, alive in his arms, and he was coming alive again too. In one easy shift she was sitting on the kitchen bench, sliding his theatre top over his head, and the moan of delight as she saw his torso had him so hard he had to slow himself down. Her fingers pressed harder into his shoulder, her hungry lips tasting his nipples now. Angus noticed there were still the last remnants of glitter on her nipple, this little glimmer of gold where there shouldn't be, and he sucked at it, yet still it stayed. He flicked at the fleck again with his tongue, willing himself to slow down, but she was playing with the ties of his theatre bottoms now, pulling them down with some difficulty over his erection as he dealt with the far easier task of her bikini bottom ties.

Alone in the kitchen, not a wedding ring between them, but there was a whole lot else. Staring into her pale blue eyes, seeing her blink, Angus knew she knew it too.

'We shouldn't…' he half heartedly attempted, kissing her again.

'We should,' Imogen purred as she kissed him back.

'You'll be gone soon…'

'I'm here now.' She guided his hands to her sweetest place and as the pad of his thumb took her most intimate pulse, he tried one last attempt at reason.

'It's too soon…' But her ankles were round his back and it felt like he'd been waiting for ever.

'Not for me.'

'I'm crazy about you, Imogen,' Angus gasped, hovering at her entrance, seeing the golden curls that beckoned him and desperate to enter, her breathless response all the invitation required as he plunged in blissfully.

'Me, too!'

It was like stumbling into paradise, feeling her legs coil around him as she dragged him in, smelling her, tasting her, feeling her. This stunning, beautiful woman was somehow as into him as much as he was into her. It *was* too much, and certainly *too soon*, and just as Angus tried to slow himself down, just as he forced himself to think about tax receipts and spreadsheets and anything mundane, she dragged him in deeper, her ankles coiling around his back, her head arching backwards, and he kissed the hollows of her throat. Angus knew that nothing was going to distract him now, and better still, as he felt her tighten, and heard these little throaty gasps come from the throat he was kissing, distraction was as unnecessary as it was impossible. He could feel the rhythm of her orgasm beating for him to join her in this heady place, and the only thing Angus was concentrating on was her, was Imogen, and how she made him feel. Then the heaven of his climax and the sheer pleasure of hers when it happened had his heart thumping a tattoo in his chest. As he held her after it all should have dimmed as reality invaded, as they were back in the kitchen having taken the biggest most reckless step of their lives. But, if anything, the world looked better.

'Oh, Angus.' Still inside her, still holding her, as blue eyes met his, there was no place he would rather have been. 'What do you do to me?'

'I could ask the same thing.'

And it should have been awkward, only it wasn't.

And guilt was curiously absent as he kissed her again.

There was not even a hint of uncertainty as she popped the pancakes in the microwave for all of thirty seconds, grabbed a fork and they both headed upstairs, just a tiny pause at the landing as he steered her to his bedroom.

'My room,' Imogen insisted. 'I can't do anything in there.'

'I can't do anything in the nanny's room!' Angus grinned. 'Anyway, it's a single bed!'

'Brilliant!'

'I thought I was getting an ulcer.'

'You need to eat more regularly.'

They were lying naked on her tiny bed, blinds closed on the skylight, the heating still up high and the radio still blaring, feeding each other mango in golden syrup, both discovering again what it felt like to be happy.

Not fine, or OK, or getting there, but actually happy.

Absolutely at ease, lost in the moment and just, well, happy.

'I keep getting this pain, you see….' Angus tapped his stomach. 'Well, not a pain as such…right here… right here in my solar plexus.'

'You poor baby!' Imogen soothed, bending her head and kissing it better.

'Every time I see your ex, either in the flesh or on the television, every time I hear Owen tell me how bloody fantastic that red-headed agency nurse is…' He blew out a breath. 'I didn't realise it at the time, but this little network of nerves, that really don't do much, scrunches into a ball every time…'

'Oh.' She looked up at him. 'Are you jealous?'

'I don't know.' Angus grimaced, because he'd never really been jealous before.

'Well, don't be!' Imogen frowned. 'Brad's like one of your boxes under the tree—beautifully gift wrapped, but sadly empty. There's nothing between us, nothing at all.'

Tired now, he watched as she slipped under the sheet, watched her lovely face on the pillow, those blue eyes smiling at him, and it felt utterly right to join her and spoon his body in behind her, to place his hand on the curve where her waist met her bottom and just hold her, and utterly wrong that in two weeks she'd be gone.

'Gemma's boyfriend's not Australian, by any chance?' Imogen said, much later in that time before falling asleep.

'Afraid not. Brad might get more work here…?'

'He's been offered a job on a children's show back home.'

'Oh.'

He wasn't remotely tired now. Too used to sleeping

alone, he had been trying to accommodate to the feel of her in his arms, trying to fathom out that this was real, as his mind, which was used to coming up with them, raced for a solution, for something, some way to hold on to what they had only just found. Only at every twist of his thoughts he was thwarted…

Kids, careers, exes, schools—oh, and a tiny matter of ten thousand or so miles.

And she waited, stared at the wall and waited for him to say that they'd work something out, waited for him to tell her that it would all be OK, that somehow it might work.

Only he couldn't.

'We should keep it quiet,' Angus said instead.

'I wasn't going to rush into work and put up a poster.'

'I know.' He felt her body stiffen, could hear the irritated edge in her voice, especially when she continued.

'Don't worry, I won't damage your perfect reputation.'

'Imogen.' He put his hand up to her cheek, tucked a stray strand of hair behind her ear and tried to voice what he was feeling. 'It's not just about my reputation—you go home soon, all it will look like to others is a fling… It's about your reputation too.'

'I know.' She was glad she was facing away from him. Tears were stinging her eyes, knowing he was right and wishing it wasn't so.

'And it would be just so confusing for the kids….'

'Of course.' She gave a big sniff. 'They don't need to know anything.' Which was right and everything, but it just made it seem like a dirty little secret. As if all they shared, all that had felt so right, was seemingly wrong.

'You know…' Imogen gave a pale smile. '…I always wondered what Heath would be like, you know, if I met someone…'

'He hasn't met any of your boyfriends?'

'There haven't been any boyfriends.'

'But you and Brad broke up ages ago.'

'I wasn't ready,' Imogen said, and he rolled her towards him then, didn't want to talk to her back when he could see her instead, and he stared deep into those eyes that had entranced him from the second they'd locked with his. He knew then that he didn't really know her at all, only *how* he wanted to. He wanted to know everything about the shy but provocative, gentle yet sexy, completely stunning woman that had greeted him on the stairs, and who had just been his. 'I don't share my mango with everyone!'

She was attempting a joke, only he wasn't smiling, the seriousness of their situation hitting home. Serious, Angus realised, because this deep, beautiful woman had trusted only him with her patched-up heart, and that was something he could never take lightly.

'Come here,' he said, as if the two centimetres that separated them in the bed was as vast as the distance that separated their future. Pulling her towards him, he kissed her deeply, though tenderly, blotting out the many questions with slow, deep answers, because for now there wasn't any rush. They didn't have to think about anything right now.

Imogen wasn't going anywhere today and neither was Angus.

CHAPTER NINE

'WHAT did you guys do today?'

'Nothing!' Looking up from smiling, pyjama-clad people mulling over a vast jigsaw, Imogen's smile was arguably the widest when Angus came home from work the next day. 'We just flopped.'

'Flopped?'

'Flopped around and didn't do much. We didn't even get dressed—did we, guys?'

'We brushed our teeth!' Jack said.

'I didn't!' Heath grinned, but one look from his mother and he hurtled up the stairs to the bathroom. Also in pyjamas, Imogen wandered into the kitchen where Angus was serving up some wicked-looking noodles.

'Thanks for this!'

'They're just noodles!'

'I mean this…' She gave a sigh of contentment as she looked around and beyond the kitchen. 'You have no idea how much it means to just do *nothing* with Heath. It's just been so nice to have a quiet day, instead of thinking up things to do or sitting in a burger bar, which is what I would have been doing today if I wasn't here.'

'Thank you too…' Angus smiled. 'It's been so nice to go to work and know the kids are happy and not have to worry about what I'm going to find when I come home. Have they asked about Gemma?'

'Clemmie has.' Imogen nodded. 'Gemma rang this afternoon and spoke to them for a couple of minutes, but Jack's asking when she's coming home. Have you spoken to her?'

'I've rung her,' Angus said, 'but I just got her voice-mail. I've sent her a few texts—told her that we need to sort things out as to what to tell the kids. I've told her too that she needs to see them…' He raked a hand through his hair. 'I'm just in this holding pattern—till I see her, till I speak to her, I don't know…'

Which left Imogen in a holding pattern too.

Knowing that at any minute Gemma could come back, that with one phone call everything would change.

And it was selfish of her to not wish that for him.

How could she not wish that his relationship with Gemma was salvageable? How could she not wish that Clemmie and Jack's mum might suddenly come home—after all, home was where she would be heading soon.

'Have you sorted out the boxroom for Heath?' His question dragged her out of her introspection. 'There are spare pillows in the hall cupboard, I think.'

'I had hoped he'd want to sleep in with me, given we haven't spent a night under the same roof for a while, but times have changed apparently—he's got new friends now!'

'There's a trundle bed under Jack's,' Angus suggested.

'All options examined…' Imogen rolled her eyes.

'They want to camp out.' She gave a little wince. 'In the lounge.'

'Of course they do!' Angus grinned and she was so happy he did—so happy that a little bit of chaos didn't matter to him. 'Why would you want a soft warm bed when there's a cold hard floor?'

'They're planning a midnight feast too.' Imogen giggled. 'Though we don't know about that.'

And she loved it that he lowered all the crisps and treats to a lower shelf, loved it that he put a few cans of usually forbidden fizz in the fridge and pulled the ice cream to the front of the freezer. Loved it that he couldn't just *get* the blankets for the kids to make the fort, but *had* to help them too. And with growing amusement Imogen came back from a long soak in the bath to find some rather impressive-looking tents, all of which Angus had to go in and check for size and comfort.

'Mine's the best!' Clemmie demanded. 'Isn't it, Imogen?'

'It's fabulous!' Imogen declared, checking it out for herself. 'I might sleep here myself.'

And later, when the living room was a no-go zone, and Imogen had eaten the last of the noodles while Angus finished off the crossword in the newspaper, when she was sitting in a dressing-gown at the kitchen table as Angus headed off to the shower, when his mother called and she had to knock for him to come out of the shower, it was just too much.

Standing in the kitchen dripping wet with a towel around his hips, trying to find a pen to write down his mother's flight arrival time, Imogen knew that if she spent a second longer in the same room with him and didn't touch him, she'd surely self combust, and she could take no more.

'I'm going to bed.'

'It's only nine o'clock!' Angus said, cursing as the crayon he was using to write, suddenly snapped. 'What did I say the flight number was?'

Only she couldn't answer. Simply couldn't tell him how much she wanted him, or how it was killing her inside to know that this magical evening doing *nothing* with the kids, this slice of heaven they had found, couldn't be shared with others and certainly couldn't last.

'I'll make you a cup of tea…' He was halfway to the kettle and she'd half decided to stay up a bit longer when the phone rang. She watched the set of his shoulders stiffen, watched his free hand rake through his damp hair and even before he said her name, Imogen knew that it was Gemma.

Knew she wouldn't be getting her cup of tea.

Closing the kitchen door, she checked on the kids— smiling at their excited faces and joining in the fun, leaving him to it, because his marriage ending had nothing to do with her.

But it was hard.

Especially when the phone in the living room clicked off and she knew the call was over, but he still didn't come out.

Especially when later, much later, the kids charged into the kitchen, with Imogen racing to stop them, only to find Angus with his head in his hands at the table.

'Are you crying?' Clemmie said accusingly.

'Don't be daft!' Angus grinned but looked distinctly glassy-eyed. 'I've got a cold.'

And later, lying in bed, she could hear the commotion downstairs, kids giggling, the fridge door opening, and as the bedroom door pushed open and he sat down on the side of her bed, she hated the tears that greeted his hand when he stroked her cheek.

'Sorry!' She shuddered the word out.

'For what?'

'You were right….' Imogen gulped. 'It is too soon.'

'Not for me.'

'You miss her—and it's right that you miss her…'

'Imogen, have you any idea how unbearable the last few days would have been without you?' Still he stroked her cheek. 'And have you any idea how unbearable my life was before I met you?'

'No.'

'She's coming over tomorrow. We're going to tell the kids—that's what's beating me up.'

'It's nearly Christmas,' Imogen croaked.

'Which gives us a little time to get our act together for Christmas Day.' Angus screwed his eyes closed. 'Couldn't she have waited?' Then he cursed himself. 'I shouldn't have pushed things—'

'No.' Imogen interrupted. 'Angus, you can't plan these things and Gemma couldn't either. She didn't just *decide* to fall in love…'

'Don't expect me to forgive her…' Angus shook his head.

'Would it have been any easier in September?' Imogen

asked. 'With Clemmie all excited about school… Or maybe you could have held out till Easter…'

'Imogen, don't…'

But she did.

'Or last year when you knew things were over…'

'No,' Angus admitted. Gazing down at her, the muddied waters cleared a touch as he realised in many ways that time had actually been kind, because somehow she was here beside him. 'What would I do without you?'

'You'll find out soon enough.'

His mouth was gentle. A kiss so tender, so kind, so merited that for that second, even if the kids had rampaged up the stairs and caught them, it would have surely been justified.

So justified that when the crisp packets were empty, when the carefully built tents had long since collapsed and three little people lay curled up on the floor, with Angus and Imogen tucking blankets around shoulders, it seemed right that he take her hand as they headed up the stairs to bed. Somehow it would be wrong to sleep alone tonight.

'Put the chair against the door.' Imogen gulped, shy all of a sudden, hating the body he seemed to adore, not as bold as before and wishing he'd turn the lights off or would turn around long enough so that she could jump under the covers without him seeing her.

But see her he did.

One touch and she was comfortable.

One kiss and he soothed her.

Chased away the insecurities with every caress.

And never had his love been as sweet as it was bitter.

The depth of his kiss almost annulled by its sheer impossibility. Like a barnacle on a rock, she clung to him, couldn't bear that soon they would be ripped apart. Her single bed was just so much better for the intimacies they shared, to feel the muscle of him beside her, every roll, every kiss, every tumble bringing them closer until he was where he belonged—inside her.

And it was the saddest, sweetest love she had ever made. Every stroke, every beat of him pushing them to a place they'd never been, to mutuality, affinity, to a space in the world that was solely for them.

Sweet to have visited.

So sad to leave.

Her single bed huge when later, much later, he crept from the room.

CHAPTER TEN

OH, YOU can smile and distract, you can make soothing noises, you can ignore and deny and you can really try to hide things, but children always know.

Especially at Christmas.

'Mum's coming in an hour.' Clemmie was sitting on the stairs, watching as Imogen pulled her boots and coat on. She was taking Heath on the London Duck Tour, would ride around Central London then plunge into the Thames in the same amphibious vehicle.

Heath had been bright-eyed with excitement when Imogen had told him about it.

Jack and Clemmie hadn't even asked if they could go.

'That's good,' Imogen said, looking at her little angry face and truly not knowing what to say.

'I'm going to play in my room.'

Imogen didn't call out goodbye to Angus and didn't call it out to the children, relieved just to open the front door and escape the oppressive atmosphere.

'Hello, Imogen.'

The camera did lie. Because standing on the door-step, close to six feet tall in high-heeled cream boots and a soft cream coat, dark hair billowing around her pale face, Imogen hadn't braced herself for Gemma's absolute beauty, or that she might know her name.

'Angus said he'd arranged some temporary help…'

Oh, she needn't have worried, Imogen realised, because not for a second would this stunning woman ever consider her a threat. It wouldn't even enter her head that Angus might want someone as dowdy and as plain as her.

'The children have raved about you on the phone… Thank you so much for taking care of my babies,' Gemma continued in a flurry, and Imogen realised the woman was actually beside herself with nerves, still standing on the doorstep of her own home, as if it was up to Imogen to ask her inside.

Truly not knowing what to say, Imogen was saved from answering as Angus came down the hallway.

'Hello, Gemma.'

'Oh, Angus.'

Of course she didn't need to be asked in, Imogen thought as she stepped out into the street. Of course, when Gemma burst out crying, Angus would comfort her as together they faced the most appalling task together. Only she had never expected to like her, had never expected to be moved by the raw tears that had spilled from her eyes, the throaty sob that had come from her lips. And if it moved her, then what must it have done for Angus?

Maybe they might make it work, Imogen thought, huddled up with Heath, freezing as they sped through the streets taking photos and quacking at passersby.

Heath whooped with delight as they plunged into the river and even though it was fun and brilliant and a day she'd remember for ever, Imogen felt as if her heart was being squeezed from the inside.

Especially after she dropped off Heath at Brad's and went back to a house that felt different somehow, no matter how Angus tried to act normal.

A new normal.

A new normal where Angus went into work for a few hours and Gemma came over on Christmas Eve to take the children out and Imogen attempted some last-minute Christmas shopping. Heath was easy to buy for and Jack and Clemmie were too. Brad? Well, thankfully, given it was December, sunglasses were drastically reduced in price, which took care of that.

If only Angus was so easy.

Along with the last of the frantic last-minute shoppers she wandered around vast department stores, trying to find the perfect present for the perfect man—and knowing she had one chance to get it right.

That this could be their only Christmas.

And it would take more than a miracle for it to be a happy one. There was just way too much hurt all around.

'Get everything?' Angus asked, when laden with bags she nearly fell through the door.

'If I didn't, it's too late now! How are the kids?' Imogen added, as he helped her stuff the bags in the stair cupboards.

'They seem OK…' His jacket and tie were off, his shirt coming untucked at the hips, but he was still the most impressive man she had ever seen, Imogen thought as he waited till they were alone before discussing it again. 'They really do seem OK. You know, we clung on for a year, thinking we were doing the right thing, but I'm starting to wonder if we—'

'My tooth fell out!' Clemmie burst into the kitchen, dripping blood and smiling at the same time.

'That's what happens if you keep tugging at it.' Angus grinned, getting a wad of kitchen roll and dealing with the casualty. 'She's hoping for bonus points if Santa and the tooth fairy both come on Christmas Eve!'

Clemmie grinned her gappy smile and it reminded Imogen so much of Heath it hurt. Oh, she adored Clemmie, adored Jack, only they weren't her babies.

Her first Christmas Eve without Heath beside her and surely no one in the world knew how she felt.

Except one.

'Mum's on the phone!' Angus called later as he was putting two excited children to bed. Imogen sat in a room bathed with fairy lights, feeling sick on her third mince pie, missing Heath so much it hurt. As she watched a rerun of Shane, all Imogen could wonder was how grown-ups got it so wrong.

How did they mess up so badly—and who was it that suffered the most?

And then she thought of Maria.

Tears sliding down her cheeks, she thought of how, even if it was a difficult life sometimes, she'd so much rather live it. She thought of little Guido, and prayed he was OK without his parents to love him. She barely looked up when Angus walked into the lounge, laden with boxes that *weren't* empty for underneath the tree.

'Still hurts, huh?' Angus asked, staring for a minute at the TV and Shane, then back at her.

'Always,' Imogen answered, as his pager trilled.

And because he was a consultant, because the pubs were turning out and because Gus had promised to come in at six next morning if he could just have Christmas Eve undisturbed, she nodded and took over.

Lugging the presents under the tree as he sped into the night.

She left the Christmas lights on and took bites out of four mince pies then bit on the carrot that had been left for Rudolph. Then she headed up the stairs and quietly filled their stockings, before having to go back down because she'd forgotten that the tooth fairy was coming tonight too. By the end it was a relief, just a blessed relief, to finally close her bedroom door.

It would take more than a miracle to make this Christmas a happy one, Imogen thought, staring up at her little skylight, hearing the wail of sirens in the distance and the swoosh of cars as they sped through the night. Finally she gave way to the tears she'd held in as she'd hung Clemmie's stocking and fiddled with Jack's; as she'd kissed two little faces goodnight, and had done all the right things for Gemma's children…

While all the while missing her own.

CHAPTER ELEVEN

THERE was one advantage to putting two overexcited children to bed on Christmas Eve.

It was actually past eight when the ringing of the phone pierced the house. Sitting up, blinking through swollen lids, Imogen *just* had time to grab her sarong and wrap it around her before two thoroughly over-excited bundles burst into her room.

'Mummy's coming!' Jack yelped. 'She's coming over!'

'Santa's been!' Clemmie chimed in.

Various squeals pierced her brain as two mini-tornadoes spun out of her room and charged down the stairs, leaving Imogen to ponder that things really did seem better in the morning as she was greeted by one tired unshaven sexy blond in a pair of hipsters.

'They seem OK with it.' She could hear the relief in his voice. 'Gemma called me at work. We're going to do Christmas dinner here.'

'That's great.'

'I'm not so sure…' Angus frowned. 'Won't it be too confusing for them?'

'They don't seem confused!' Imogen said, and then

looked at him, really looked at him, because Angus didn't seem confused either. The tense man she had met that first day, the strained man she had seen on the day everything had fallen apart, seemed light years away from the one who stood before her now. 'Merry Christmas, Angus.'

'It looks like we might just manage to scrape one together,' Angus answered. 'Merry Christmas, Imogen.'

Standing on the landing with a lovely soft mouth that thoroughly kissed her, and a morning erection that had them both wondering if they could leave it to the kids to find out what Santa had bought them, while Daddy and Imogen concentrated on being naughty and nice, it actually started to look like it might be.

'When did you get back?' Imogen asked directly into his mouth.

'Seven.' His mouth answered into her kiss.

'Daddy!' Clemmie wailed from downstairs.

Christmas really was magic.

Imogen had seen it in her training when she'd worked a shift on the children's ward—seen how, no matter how dire, everyone pulled together and made the impossible work on that day. She'd seen it in her own family a few short years ago and was seeing it now with Angus's.

Angus, with an hour's sleep to his name, trying to work out what parcel Santa had left for whom, because he'd been sure when he'd wrapped them that he'd remember! Smiling and holding it together and doing his very best for the two little people who mattered most.

Or rather three little people.

Imogen pulled out her phone and chatted excitedly

to Heath, who was ripping open parcels of his own, and then to Brad, instructing him to turn down the turkey and telling him that she'd be there by ten.

And Gemma must be feeling the same, because she rang again, laughing and talking to the kids and reminding them she'd be there by eleven.

And by the time the kids were whizzing around the room, building Lego castles and playing with dolls, Angus had his little pile of presents left to open and Imogen was blinking at her rather big pile.

A big pile she truly hadn't been expecting.

'Go on, then!' Angus prompted.

'You first,' Imogen replied, just wanting to get it over, kicking herself at the choice she'd made, of all the stupid, soppy, romantic things to go and buy him.

Not that Angus thought it was.

'A waffle-maker?' She could hear the sort of bafflement in his voice as he stared at his kitchen appliance.

'It's going to be your new best friend.' Imogen smiled. 'Brilliant for a quick lunch, or a nice breakfast for the kids…sort of like a pancake mixture…' She saw a smile flare at the side of his mouth as he examined his gift rather more closely.

'Heart-shaped waffles!' Angus said.

'And they only take a few moments to make!'

She saw his tongue roll in his cheek, saw the shake of his head as he got it—all the hours searching for the perfect gift more than worth it now, her humour his.

His loss hers.

'It looks like I'm going to be eating a lot of waffles when you're…'

He didn't say it, he didn't have to—they both knew what lay ahead. And Imogen actually got it then—she'd been waiting, waiting for the wave of grief to hit him, and she realised then that it already had. That hellish year he had lived through had been his mourning time, and Angus really was ready to move on.

It nearly killed her that it wouldn't be with her.

'From the kids!' Angus said, as she opened her smellies.

'From me…' he said gruffly, as she pulled back the wrapper on a vast silk bedspread. 'I'll pay the excess baggage—figured if I can't be with you…'

And it was so nice…too nice, just a whole world away where she'd have to cuddle up to this instead of him, it was easier to open her next present than to think about it.

'From me too…' Angus said as she unwrapped a beautiful glass snow globe, shaking it up and watching the snow fall on Knightsbridge.

'I can see the food hall!' Imogen joked, pretending to peer into the tiny windows. 'Ooh, mangoes!'

'Keep opening.'

'There's more? Angus you shouldn't have…'

'I didn't. You seem to have built up quite a fan club since you've been here.'

'Lollies?'

'Sweets in England!' Angus grinned. 'Read the card.'

> *Dear Imogen,*
> *I asked Elise to drop these off for you and your lovely little boy.*

I felt awful at first being so helpless, but Elise said she doesn't mind a bit!!!
   Enjoy being spoiled.
   I do!
   Ivy Banford

'Cheeky old thing!' Imogen grinned, but her eyes were brimming. 'What's this?' she asked, turning over a silver envelope.

'I'm not sure. I saw Heather putting it in the agency nurse's pigeon hole and I swiped it for you.'

'Probably just a card from Heather…'

But it wasn't. She barely made it past the first line…handing it to Angus who after a moment read it out loud.

   'Dear Imogen,

   'You spent time with my sister when I could not. Maria worried about her house, she told me you understood—that meant a lot to her—to be understood on that day.

   'Forgive me if you find this gift offensive—my hope is to make you smile as you think of my sister.

   'With deepest thanks,

   'Elijah and Guido Vanaldi'

'That's quite a fan club you've got there,' Angus said, his voice just a touch gruff, reading the gift card more closely. 'You have a cleaner for a year.'

'A cleaner?'

'Actually, you have the crème de la crème of cleaners, to do with what you will for a year… What sort of a present is that?'

'The perfect one.' Imogen crumpled. 'Only I won't be here…'

And she truly didn't know if she was crying because she'd miss him and the children or crying because right now she missed Heath, or crying for Maria, or for the fact that the one time in her life she had the crème de la crème of *everything* lined up and at her service and raring to go, she was in absolutely no position to take what was on offer.

'Come on…' Angus summoned her to the kitchen. 'We've got cooking to do.'

Jack, wearing reindeer ears, poured the batter, and Clemmie insisted on being chief taster. Breakfast really was delicious, but as wonderful as it was to be with Angus, Jack and Clemmie on Christmas morning, there was somewhere else she needed to be.

Wanted to be.

'I'm going to go.'

It was barely after nine, but long before that he had sensed her distraction, knew she wanted to be with Heath. Watched as she applied mascara, lipstick, pulled on her boots, hugged the kids and told them to have a great day.

Watched as she left.

Then waited for Gemma to arrive.

And Christmas really was magic, because somehow he wasn't quite so angry. Somehow he managed to just put it all on hold.

He had understood when he'd seen Gemma's puffy

eyes and nervous face that she had been scared—scared of facing him, scared of telling the kids, scared of the future too, no doubt.

So they had one thing in common at least! And now they had two, both wanting to give their kids a good Christmas to remember.

'Wow!' Gemma beamed as the kids showed her the graffiti job they'd performed on the tree. 'You two have been busy!'

'Imogen helped us make them.'

'Imogen?' She glanced over to Angus. 'The kids do seem fond of her. Can she stay on?'

'Afraid not!' Angus busied himself picking up wrapping paper. 'But Mum's coming in a couple of days and I'll put an ad in in the new year.'

'Well, between us all…' Gemma was picking up paper too, holding a garbage bag for the first time in years and actually cleaning up the mess so they could enjoy the day '…we'll work it all out.'

Yes, magic, because when, after a vast Christmas dinner and a couple of very welcome glasses of Imogen's red wine, he didn't explode when Gemma asked if she could have the children with her that night where she was staying.

'You're staying with him?'

'Yes, but he's not there tonight—he's going to visit his family. I thought it might be better for the children to see where I'm staying for the first time without Roger being there…' She swallowed hard as she voiced his name. 'I think that would be too confusing for them.'

Oh, and there was such a smart retort on the tip of

his tongue, but he swallowed it down with another swig of wine and managed a curt nod.

Magic, because later, when the house was unbearably quiet, when the living room was littered with toys and no kids, and all the beds upstairs were empty, when for a second he didn't think he could stand it, there she was. He watched from the window as Brad dropped Imogen off, grimacing just a touch as she kissed her ex goodbye. In turn Imogen sniffed Gemma's perfume in the air when she walked through the door.

'How was it?'

'Great!' Imogen beamed, depositing a large amount of bags, not noticing the set of his jaw as she opened a box and pulled out a pair of soft suede boots. 'He remembered my size.'

'How's Heath?'

'Asleep!' Imogen giggled. 'Not for long, though. With the amount of cake and drinks he's had, I wouldn't be surprised if he's up a few times in the night. But we had a great day. I was so worried how it would be, but it turned out to be wonderful. How about for you?'

'It went pretty well,' Angus said, 'given the circumstances. We just put everything on hold and tried to give the kids a great day—which I think we did.'

'Are they in bed?'

'They're at Gemma's.' He saw her eyes widen just a fraction. 'They really did seem to have a good day. They're going to stay again in a couple of nights if all goes well. They went about half an hour before you came home.' She watched him flinch at his choice of words and gave a soft smile.

'It feels like home.' Imogen said, because it did. Getting out of the car and walking up the steps, for the first time in the longest time she actually felt as if she was coming home. This peace to her soul that he brought, a connection that was blissfully familiar. 'And well done, you.'

Yes, it felt like home and it felt like Christmas when, full from the day's excesses, they still managed to gorge on Ivy's presents as they sat cuddled up on the sofa beside the twinkling Christmas tree, watching the same slushy movie that was surely on the world over on Christmas night. It felt like home and it felt completely right.

So right it hurt.

CHAPTER TWELVE

'I'M SCARED.'

At three in the morning and after a long and exhausting labour, Roberta Cummings had every reason to be scared. Her labour hadn't progressed but, determined to deliver naturally, she had held on. Imogen had come in often to check and finally the resident had sent for his registrar when, at still only five centimetres dilated, the baby's heart rate had started to dip during contractions and an emergency caesarean had been decided on.

'You're going to be fine.' Imogen assured Roberta.

'What about the baby?'

'Hey!' Imogen held the terrified woman's hand and it was such bliss to be able to reassure her, 'We've been watching you closely all night and we're doing this now, *before* the baby gets into too much distress… When you wake up, you'll have your baby!'

There was a quiet assuredness in Imogen, which she imbued in her patients. Here on Maternity, even though things could go wrong, even though they did, Imogen was confident in the process of birth, even when it was a complicated one. With the right team and the right approach, this emergency would turn into something wonderful and *that* for Imogen made it the place she wanted to be.

'Now, do you understand what's happening?' Smiling down at his patient, despite the flurry of activity going on in the theatre, the obstetrician, Oliver Hanson, was calm and unruffled. 'We can't wait for the epidural to take effect, so the anaesthetist is going to put you to sleep…'

'Think baby thoughts.' Imogen smiled as the anaesthetist placed a mask over Roberta's face, and Imogen held her hand, watched her relax and then stiffen. Then, as medications were slipped into her IV, she jolted as her body resisted, and then relaxed again as the anaesthetist swiftly intubated.

'Let's get this little guy out,' Oliver said. Only now, with the patient safely asleep, did he show the haste this procedure required if the baby was to be born safely. Making his incision, strong arms had to work hard as the baby's head was deep into the birth canal. A wrinkly purple bottom followed by two floppy legs was delivered onto the drapes, and even though it was the third delivery Imogen had seen that night, still it never ceased to amaze her. She watched as he was expertly lifted, a theatre nurse receiving the precious bundle and heading over to the cot as the team vigorously rubbed the baby, his navy eyes open, not even blinking.

'Let's cover that ugly head before Dad sees you!' Rita, a senior midwife said with a laugh as the baby's head was elongated from his difficult attempt at birth.

They all knew it would all settle down soon, but could often scare new parents. 'Right, Imogen, do you want to take him to the nursery?'

Which was the best bit for Imogen, introducing the little fellow to his dad, who sat and held him as they waited for his mum to be ready to meet him too. Oh, and she could have bathed him and dressed him up in one of the little outfits his mum had brought in for this day, but she chose to wait and let Roberta see him all sticky and messy and covered in vernix.

'Imogen?' Rita popped her head in just as Imogen was introducing a very tired but elated Roberta to her son. 'The nurse co-ordinator's on the telephone. Now that we've quietened down here, she wondered if you'd mind popping down to Emergency for the last couple of hours of your shift.'

'Sorry about this!' Heather apologised the moment Imogen hit the department and she walked her over to Resus. 'The place is steaming. I had to send two staff home at midnight with this wretched flu that's going around—that's why I'm stuck on nights too—then we had this one bought in…

'Gunshot wound!' she added as they walked briskly. 'To the right upper chest, and from what the police say there might be a couple more on the way!'

'Can we roll him over?' Angus didn't acknowledge her and she didn't expect him to as she joined the rather sparse trauma team and helped to roll the patient over so that Angus could examine the exit wound. She knew she was just another pair of efficient hands as they raced to put in a chest drain and push through blood in the hope of getting him up to Theatre before he bled out. For the second time that night Imogen hit the theatre doors, running alongside Angus, the thoracic team having run ahead and already scrubbed and gotten in place.

'Sorry!' Both slightly breathless from the run and adrenaline, it took a while for Imogen to answer.

'For what?' Imogen stopped at the water cooler and took a long drink. 'I don't expect you to kiss me hello!'

'For telling Heather to get you from Maternity.'

'You told Heather that I was working?' Imogen frowned.

'I said that I'd bumped into you in the car park.' Registering her frown, he spectacularly misinterpreted it. 'It was hardly the place to say that I knew you were at work.'

'I'm not worried about that.' Stopping midway in the corridor she angrily confronted him. 'I was actually enjoying my shift. I assumed that the nurse co-ordinator had requested me. You had no right to tell them to pull me off Maternity.'

'Imogen, a guy was bleeding out. We had staff dropping like flies and Heather frantically trying to call people in. I *knew* that there was an experienced emergency nurse up on Maternity. We needed you—'

'Needed me?' Imogen furiously interrupted. 'Or was it just terribly convenient that I happened to be there?'

'Well done, guys!' Heather's weary face greeted two stony ones. 'Thanks so much for that, Imogen—I don't know what we'd have done without you.'

'Survived, no doubt!'

'Probably.' Heather yawned. 'But you made things a lot easier. Hey, Angus, I was going to drop round this afternoon when I woke up. I've made up a few meals…'

'You don't have to do that.' Angus smiled and shook his head. 'Anyway, I'm going to the airport to pick up Mum.'

'Well, tomorrow, then,' Heather pushed. 'I can pop them over—'

'And offend my mum!' Angus's smile froze in his face as he met Imogen's eyes. 'Honestly, Heather, we're fine. You don't have to worry.'

'You were right.' Angus arrived home a couple of hours after Imogen, and she could have pretended to be asleep but couldn't be bothered with games. Instead, she just lay there as Angus placed a mug of tea on her bedside table and nudged her knees just a little bit to make room for him when he sat down. 'I shouldn't have told Heather that you were working— I should have left it to the co-ordinator to work it out. I just didn't think. The department was bursting and we needed help quickly…'

'I get all of that,' Imogen said, staring up at the skylight, 'but don't…' blue eyes snapped to his '…choose when it's convenient to know me.'

'I don't.'

'Come on, Angus. You're not leaving for the airport till five—don't tell me if I wasn't here that Heather wouldn't be welcome to drop over.'

'I don't need food parcels, Imogen.'

'Perhaps, but if Heather drops by and sees me here,

then work will know, which wouldn't look too good for you, would it?'

'What do you want me to say here?' Angus asked. 'That we should tell everyone? Tell them at work, tell Gemma, tell my mother, tell the kids… And then what? You'll go. You'll be on that plane and back to your life in Australia and I'll still be here. Surely it's better if it's just between us.'

'Which is why I think I should go. I don't think it can work with your mum here. I think it might be awkward…' Imogen gulped. 'I mean, it's hard enough keeping it from the kids.'

'She doesn't still tuck me in at night.' Angus attempted a joke, only she didn't return his smile.

'It's not about that…' Tears were welling in her eyes. 'It's about us. I mean, she'll know I'm not the nanny or just a friend helping out. She'll see what we're like….'

'Like what?'

'Like this.'

And she answered the question that he hadn't been able to back at the café. When she'd asked him what the different things had been that he and Gemma had wanted, he hadn't known how to answer, but *this* was what he wanted and *this* was what he couldn't have.

'Stay.' He didn't know if he was asking for the next few nights or for ever, but he knew her answer covered both.

'I can't.'

'Don't go.' His eyes closed on the impossibility of it all, then opened again, his voice firmer now. 'Look, I've got to pick up the kids at three. Come to the airport, stay for a couple of days, at least till after New Year. You can't stay at the hostel for that…'

'I might want to go out partying!' Imogen tried, but they both knew she wouldn't.

'Stay a bit longer and let the kids get used to the idea of you going…'

'They're not going to miss me….'

'Oh, they will.' Angus insisted. 'I can assure you my mum won't notice a thing. And if by some miracle she does…' he blew out a breath '…then I guess I'll have to just deal with it.'

'You're so pretty!' Clemmie sighed as, feeling anything but, Imogen peered in the mirror at her puffy face and dragged a brush through her hair.

'Really? Well, so are you.'

'Oh, I will be,' Clemmie nodded assuredly, 'when my teeth stop falling out.'

They were just adorable.

Used to dealing with kids, it still took her by surprise how quickly she'd come to *like* Clemmie and Jack. Oh, all kids were cute and all kids were nice and funny if you stopped to look, but too many years in Emergency had knocked some of that sentiment out of her.

Till she'd had Heath and till she'd met Clemmie and Jack.

Jack, as direct and as serious as his father could be.

Clemmie, as offbeat and as funny as her father could sometimes be too!

And she adored them both for it—for the way they'd made Heath feel welcome, for the tiny moments like this one as Clemmie stood in the bathroom and told Imogen she was wonderful then promptly steered the conversation back to herself.

'I wish I could look pretty for the party tomorrow.'

'That's right.' Imogen smothered a smile as Clemmie worked her way up to whatever it was she'd be asking. 'You and Jack have got a party to go to.'

'I don't want Nanny to do my hair.' Clemmie came over and fiddled with her hairbrush. 'She hurts when she brushes it and she doesn't do it very nice—she always puts it in bunches. But if you're my nanny too...'

'I'm not really a nanny, and your Nanny's a different sort of nanny...' Imogen attempted, but it was too hard. 'But, yes, I am helping look after you and, if you want, I can do your hair.'

'With that sparkly stuff that was in my stocking?' Clemmie checked, finally getting to the point she had been wanting to make all along!

'Sure.' Imogen grinned.

The drive to the airport was pretty fraught, the traffic moving at a snail's pace, giving Angus and Imogen plenty of time to pause for thought as they watched the planes take off and land. Three weeks had stretched endlessly ahead, when Imogen had first landed. A long, long holiday then she'd go back home with Heath. At first it had felt like for ever, only now, as all good holidays do at the end, the days were starting to fly by fast. New Year's Eve was just around the corner and then just a few days after she would be on her way home.

She'd made so many plans, there had been so many

things she'd wanted to do in her time here, and she'd achieved them all—just never when she'd made those plans had she expected to fall in love.

Yes, love.

Oh, she'd told herself it was a holiday romance, only that didn't quite fit.

Holiday romances didn't work, apparently because you were lying on a beach by day getting nice and tanned and out at night sipping cocktails, which didn't translate to the real world.

Yet they'd lived in the real world.

Through the rain and the gloom they'd still managed to find laughter, so it couldn't be a holiday romance. And it certainly wasn't a fling…at least not for her.

Heathrow was as daunting as it had been when she'd arrived with Heath—people everywhere, trolleys, noise, tension, and that was just the car park! But standing in Arrivals she couldn't help but get caught up in the excitement. Clemmie, dancing on the spot, arguing with Jack as to what presents Nanny might bring. Imogen wondered what Angus's mother would be like. She imagined some stern, serious, forebidding-looking woman and reeled a touch when all four feet eleven of Jean was introduced to her. Imogen realised before they'd even made it back to the car that Angus's mother was completely potty and really quite lovely.

'Could you make me a cup of tea?' She smiled sweetly at Imogen as they stepped into the house and Angus baulked.

'I told you, Mum, she's not a housekeeper. Imogen's a friend who's helping out.'

'Then she won't mind making me a cup of tea!'

'I don't mind at all,' Imogen answered, smothering a smile as she filled the teapot.

'She'll be back soon!' Jean said, as if Gemma had gone on day trip.

'It's over, Mum.'

'Marriage takes work, Angus.'

'And we did work at it.'

'It wasn't all perfect for your father and I. But we worked at it.'

'Mum, Gemma's met someone else.'

'Maybe she's got that postnatal depression or something.'

'Give me strength!' Angus gritted his teeth as Jean headed off to the bathroom. 'Clemmie's four!'

'She just doesn't want it to be over.'

'But it is.' Angus gave a wry shake of his head. 'Why am I the only one who believes it?'

Still, as delightful as Jean was, as nice as dinner was, as Imogen lay in bed that night she knew there'd be no getting up for a glass of water. Knew Angus was right, that it would be unfair on Jean to tell her, unfair on the kids…. It was just unfair all round.

That glimpse of Heathrow airport, just too real to ignore, meant she couldn't pretend it wasn't happening any more.

CHAPTER THIRTEEN

'Sorry, no, I've actually got plans for New Year's Eve!' Imogen snapped off the phone just a little pink in the face as Angus knew she was lying.

'What are they?' Angus asked.

'Bath and bed!'

'Go on,' Angus pushed, 'I'm working it. It would be fun.'

'New Year's Eve in Accident and Emergency really isn't my idea of a fun night. Now, if they offered me Maternity, I might consider it.'

'Morning! Anything I can do?' Not quite so potty, Jean had retired to bed when it was time to do the dishes, had woken only after the children had eaten breakfast and was now pouring a drink from the pot of tea Imogen had just made.

'Did you hear the kettle, Mum?' Angus grinned, as Imogen's mobile shrilled again.

'Go on.' He smiled. 'It will pay for Madame Tussaud's.'

He wasn't smiling a moment later when he saw her face pale.

'Talk about what, Brad?' Imogen said as she stood up and left the room. For Angus it was almost impossible to carry on chatting to his mother as if nothing was happening. It was hell for him to just sit there and drink tea and pretend it didn't matter that for the first time since he'd known her she'd left the room to take Brad's call.

'I have to go out,' she said when she came back.

'Problem?' Angus asked, his face as strained as hers and both trying not to show it. 'Is Heath OK?'

'Heath's fine.' Imogen gave a tight shrug. 'Brad's got something he wants to discuss. I should only be a couple of hours—I'll be back in time to do Clemmie's hair.'

'Who's Brad?' Jean frowned, the second Imogen had gone.

'Imogen's ex-husband.' Funny, that of all the new phrases he'd been getting used to these past couple of weeks, that one came out the hardest.

'Nice that they're civil.'

She must be becoming a local, Imogen briefly thought as she raced up the escalator instead of just standing. She hadn't even noticed the other passengers on the tube, had just sat there staring blindly out of the darkened windows, trying to fathom what Brad could possibly have to say. Oh, he'd pulled out more than a few surprises in their time together, and a few in their time apart. She'd considered herself quite unshockable where Brad was concerned, till now.

She'd never heard him so nervous.

Laid-back Brad, suddenly supremely polite and, yes, definitely nervous.

He'd met someone, Imogen decided, taking the lift up to his apartment, just like she had… Only that wouldn't faze Brad! But maybe this one *was* serious… Maybe, Imogen gulped, this one was pregnant and there was going to be a brother or sister for Heath.

Knocking on his door, Imogen blew out her breath, sure she'd covered all options.

'Hey!' He kissed her on the cheek, just as he always did, and she played with Heath for a few moments, just as she always did, then Brad asked Heath if he'd play in his room for a moment because Mum and Dad had something they wanted to talk about.

'I don't know how to say this…' Brad wasn't his usual laid-back self as, instead of lounging on the sofa opposite he stood up and paced. 'Actually, I don't even know if I should say this. But if I don't tell you…'

Oh, she hadn't covered all her options, Imogen realised, sitting on the sofa, listening to what he had to say and realising that even after all this time Brad still had it in him to surprise her.

They were *extremely* civil, Angus thought darkly, sitting in an empty lounge, trying not to notice the semi-darkness, trying not to care that two hours had turned into six.

Only he did care.

A lot.

To ring or not?

For the hundredth time he picked up the phone, and for the hundredth time he replaced it and stared out of the window as if willing her to appear.

She'd gone to see Brad for a couple of hours, six

hours ago. She'd told Clemmie she'd be back to do her hair for the party—but she hadn't been. Clemmie was at the party wearing Jean's bunches, though Angus had managed to avoid tears by spraying them silver.

Would it look like he was checking up on her?

Was he checking up on her?

But what if she was hurt?

What if something had happened and he hadn't rung, hadn't rung because he didn't know if he was allowed to check up on her.

Seeing Brad's car pull up, seeing her pale face as she climbed out huddled in her coat, Angus's load didn't lighten. He could see the set of her shoulders, could see as she came up the steps the tension in her pale face, and as she turned the key in the door, some-how he knew it wasn't going to be great. Even before he saw her tear-streaked face and eyes that couldn't quite look at him, he knew that she had something dif-ficult to tell him.

'I'm sorry I didn't get back earlier.'

'It's fine.'

'Was Clemmie OK?'

'She's fine too. Mum's taken them to the party...' He managed a smile. 'I had a go with the sparkly stuff.'

'I wanted to ring...' Still she couldn't look at him. 'Only I didn't know what to say.'

'That's OK...'

'Brad kind of sprang something on me, something I wasn't expecting...'

And it was Angus who didn't know what to say now, Angus who really just didn't.

'I need to think, Angus.' Now she did look at him, tears pooling in her eyes. 'I know you must think—'

'I don't know what to think Imogen.'

'We were just talking about things.'

'What things?' His candid question was merited, and she looked up into those questioning jade eyes and it would have been the easiest thing in the world to tell him, to reveal to him her quandary, to ask this knowledgeable, strong man if maybe, just maybe he could show her the way. Only Imogen knew she had to find the answer herself, had learnt long ago that the easy option often turned out to be hardest in the end.

'What would you call this?' She saw his perplexed expression at her strange response. 'Us,' she elaborated. 'A fling, a relationship, a holiday romance? I mean, if you had to describe it…' The pause was interminable. Watching, waiting for him to answer, seeing the hesitation, the indecision gave Imogen the first taste of bitterness. 'But, then, you wouldn't have to describe it, because no one knows about us, do they?' She stared at him for the longest time. 'Is there any chance for you and Gemma?'

'I've already told you.' His answer came readily this time. 'We're finished.'

'Because if there is a chance,' Imogen said, ignoring his response, 'then you need to explore every option and I don't think you can do that while we're together…'

'Who are we talking about here, Imogen?' Angus asked. 'Do you really think I would have embarked on this if my marriage wasn't completely over?'

'This what, Angus?'

And he didn't know what to call it because it wasn't a fling and it wasn't some knee-jerk response to freedom either and it certainly wasn't a holiday romance, because he was right here at home and Imogen had been there for him during the most difficult of times.

Yet it couldn't be love, because if this was love, then very soon he was going to lose it, and out of all of this, it was the thing he couldn't stand losing the most. Couldn't risk loving her, only to lose her.

'Brad and I have some things that we need to sort out, and so do you and Gemma.'

He didn't even have it in him to be angry, even when later Brad's car pulled up to collect her, because as Heath thundered in and Brad waited in the car for her, though Imogen wasn't crying, she was the saddest, most confused he'd ever seen her.

It should have been easy too, for the kids to all say goodbye. Used to comings and goings, surely people who'd been in their lives for only a couple of weeks shouldn't hurt so much to lose. But they'd been through a lot together, and three tearful children didn't help matters.

'You can write…' Angus attempted.

'I can't write,' Clemmie wailed.

'Well, you can ring then.' His eyes met Imogen's. Maybe she was right to just go, because if two weeks hurt like this, imagine what it would be like in three?

'Ring me!' He fiddled with the buttons on her coat. 'I might see you at work.' He managed a weak smile. 'I promise not to haul you off Maternity again.'

'You can!' Imogen said. 'I'll call you—before I go back, I mean.'

'Do.' He didn't care if his mother was there and if he might have to explain later, didn't really care about anything, except that she was going, and he pulled her into him. Despite her bulk when he held her close, because he couldn't bear to let her go, never had someone felt more fragile.

'He's not worth it.' For the first time he crossed the line, entered a discussion where he didn't belong. 'He'll let you down.'

'I have to think,' Imogen mumbled into his shoulder, then pulled away, 'and so do you.'

CHAPTER FOURTEEN

'READY for action?'

Smiling, even though it was false, Angus walked into the staffroom at ten minutes to nine, depositing a couple of cakes and bottles of fizz on the table as he greeted the team that would witness probably the busiest of nights on the Accident and Emergency calendar year.

Oh, Christmas Eve was impossible once the pubs closed, and Christmas Day always managed to pull a few unpleasant surprises out of the hat, but the fireworks that heralded the new year weren't exclusive to the London skies. Come midnight the department, or rather the patients, would, no doubt, put on a spectacular display of their own, and extra security guards had been rostered on along with the most experienced medical staff.

'Ready!' Heather grinned—a true emergency nurse who was actually looking forward to the night. 'I've bought in a vast turkey curry—it's in the fridge, just help yourself!'

'Oh, I will!' Angus agreed, doing just that and picking up a couple of mince pies to get him started. The mood was festive almost, and although he'd brought food in and would join in with the crazy, alternative New Year's Eve party the staff would have—every breath hurt.

Hurt because a year that needed to end was about to.

Another year was starting, only he didn't quite feel ready.

He would have, though.

If Imogen hadn't entered his life.

If she hadn't waltzed right in and given him a taste of how good, how wonderful, how normal and just delicious being good and wonderful and normal could be.

He was supposed to be busy getting divorced at this point.

Not nursing a broken heart for someone else.

'Have a slice now.' Barb, one of the nurses misread his watery gaze and pushed a massive pavlova towards him, lashings of meringue laced with sugared mango. 'Imogen gave me the recipe.'

How long would it last?

How much longer would her name pepper the department? She'd worked a few shifts and it was as if she'd left a flurry of glitter wherever she'd been.

And he didn't want it to diminish.

Didn't want to take down the Christmas tree, even though Jean kept telling him to.

Didn't want to forget, even though it hurt to remember.

'Go on, have a piece—you know you want to.'

Oh, he did want to. Wanted to ring her up and tell her to get the hell away from Brad. That he didn't deserve her, had hurt her once and would do it again. But what right did he have to do that?

Except that he loved her.

Right there and then Angus admitted to himself what he didn't want to. Didn't want to love her, because he knew he was going to lose her.

They'd both known from the start that it could never go anywhere, that circumstances, geography would keep them apart but, apart or not, Angus knew he didn't need her name to be mentioned to remember the morning they'd found each other. In fact, kneed in the groin with longing, Angus knew that he'd never look at another morning without remembering her.

'Hi, guys!'

Her voice was just utterly unexpected, like some auditory hallucination as he bit into the pavlova.

'Imogen—thank heavens!' Heather practically fell on her as she walked in the staffroom just as the team headed out for handover. 'I begged the agency to send you—I had two of my senior staff ring in sick for this shift just before I went home this morning. I was desperate.'

'The agency said—the *third* time they called!' He watched as she smiled, as she deposited a vast tray on the coffee-table, kebab sticks spiked with pineapples, strawberries, kiwi fruits and mango—bringing summer into the room in so many ways. As she gave him a tight smile, blinking rapidly a few times, he knew that this was hard for her too.

Knew she didn't want to be here—but he was so glad that she was.

'Grab a drink and bring it round,' Heather ordered. 'We'll be having our coffee breaks at the nurses' station tonight. And I am sorry,' she added, 'for pestering you.'

'It worked.' Imogen smiled.

'Still, I shouldn't have asked them to ring you at the hostel when you wouldn't answer your mobile.'

And for a minute it was just the two of them. Imogen dunking a tea bag in her cup and heaping in sugar as Angus fiddled with his stethoscope.

'How have things been?'

'Good,' came her noncommittal answer.

'I didn't expect to see you tonight.'

'I didn't expect to be here, but the agency kept ringing…'

'You're staying at the youth hostel?'

'Where else would I be?' Imogen started, and then paused, two little spots of red burning in her cheek, not from embarrassment but anger. 'You think I'm back with Brad?'

'Well, you did go to him.' All the anger, all the hurt and the bitterness was there in his sentence.

'To talk…' Her words were as laced with anger and bitterness as his. 'I told you that we had things to discuss. Do you really think I'm so available that he could just snap his fingers and I'd run back?'

'Of course not.'

'That I'm so lucky to have him want me—'

'Imogen…' Angus broke in, but she didn't want to hear it.

'I told you it was over with him. I don't change my mind about things Angus…' She gave a twisted smile. 'Except when the blasted agency keep ringing and I end up doing a shift in the last place I want to be.'

'I'm sorry things are so awkward between us.'

'It's actually not all about you, Angus…' She gave a pale smile as Angus frowned. 'I'd better get round there.'

The department was fairly quiet, as it often was early on New Year's Eve, almost as if everyone saved their dramas for later. Heather made sure that her staff took themselves off for extended breaks and filled themselves up on the mountain of food they had brought, while they still had the chance. Imogen wished they were busy, wished the lull would end so the night would be over more quickly.

Wished she knew what Angus was thinking when she caught him looking at her.

'We've got a paediatric arrest coming in!' Angus's face was grim. 'Drowning.'

'Now?' It was a stupid comment. People didn't plan their dramas, didn't know that they were supposed to be quiet till midnight, and it certainly wouldn't enter the family's head that their desperately ill child was the very last thing Imogen wanted to deal with right now.

'New Year's Eve party…' Heather came off the phone from a further update from Ambulance Control. 'The bath was filled with ice for the drinks, and he fell in. Dad found him—it was his party. They can't get hold of his mum—apparently she's working tonight. We don't know how long he's been down.'

'How old?' Imogen croaked.

'Three or four,' Heather answered, 'I can't get a clear answer, it sounds pretty chaotic.'

'It's not Heath.' He could see her hands shaking as

she pulled out the leads for the cardiac monitor and opened the pads for the defibrillator, knew exactly what she was thinking.

'You don't know that.'

And he put his arm around her and gave her a squeeze, because now he could, Imogen realised, because now she'd been there a little while longer, now she was considered one of them, it was deemed appropriate.

Only it wasn't.

A friendly cuddle from him was the last thing she needed tonight.

'I'm going to wait for the ambulance,' she said, slipping his arm off and heading outside, shivering as she heard the sirens draw closer, trying to make small talk with a chatty security guard as the nine hours left of her shift stretched on endlessly.

It wasn't Heath.

The second the ambulance doors opened, her mind was put at ease, but the dread stayed with her as she took over the cardiac massage as the paramedics unclipped the stretcher and ran in. Drowning she was more familiar with than burns—nearly every garden in Australia had a pool, and sadly, and all too often, this type of patient presented.

'He's in VF...' The paramedics reeled off the list of treatment and drugs that had been given at the scene and en route, and even though it looked dire, the news was actually as good as it could be.

He was two, not three or four, Imogen heard as she pressed the palm of her hand on his sternum, and an ice-filled bath a far better option for an unsupervised toddler to tumble into than a hot one. He'd have been plunged into hypothermia, which meant the demand for oxygen to his brain would have been rapidly diminished, which gave him a better chance of being left without brain damage. He was still in VF, which meant there was some activity happening in his little heart too.

All of this went through her head as she continued the massage, stepping back every now and then as Angus shocked the little body…blocking out the cries and shouts of his family from the other side of the doors and focussing on the little boy who was clinging to life.

'Do you want to swap?' Barb offered to take over the massage, but she was getting a good rhythm on the monitor and Imogen shook her head.

'I'm fine.'

'Let's go again…' The defibrillator was whirring and Imogen felt as if she were watching from above, could see the warmed fluids dripping into his veins, could see herself going through the painful motions, and later saw the relief on everyone's face when they got him back. And, yes, she had said the right thing when she comforted the parents as Angus gave them the tentative good news and, yes, she did all the right things as she took the little boy up to the Intensive Care and handed him over. But as she walked out of the paediatric section and past the adults, she could see the bed where Maria had been, only with another person in it. And as she walked down the corridor and back to Emergency, all she knew was that she didn't want to make that walk again.

'You look exhausted!' Heather grinned as she came back. 'The night hasn't even started!'

'Fifteen minutes till lift-off!' Imogen glanced at her watch and smiled back.

'Why don't you have a break?' Heather suggested kindly. 'Take the lift and go out on the fire escape…'

'The fire escape?'

'You'll get a good view of the fireworks—if anyone deserves to see London at its best tonight, it's you.'

'This is my last shift in Emergency.' She didn't turn her head when Angus walked out onto the fire escape to join her, had seen him look up when Heather had been talking, had known that he would come.

'Your last?' The cold air caught in his throat, making it hard to keep his voice light. 'So you're ready for home, then?'

'I meant…' Her face was pale, her eyes like glass in the darkness as she turned to him. 'It's my last ever shift in Emergency. I can't do it any more. I'm going back to midwifery. I know you can't always guarantee the out-come, but I'm going to work with the lowest-risk mums and hopefully spend the rest of my nursing time bringing in lives instead of watching them end. I just can't do it any more. I can't go home and cry myself to sleep, I can't stand all the violence and the death, I just…' She shook her head. 'I just haven't got it in me any more.'

And Angus realised then, that no matter how much he might love her, he didn't really know her. That as close as they had been, there hadn't been time to get close enough, because this beautiful, talented, consummate professional actually bled inside every day she came to work.

'You're burnt out,' Angus said softly. 'It happens. Maybe take a break, do something else for a while.'

'I was hoping to do that here, only once they find out you're emergency trained...' she gave a tight smile '...well, you've seen first hand what happens.'

'I'm sorry.'

'Don't be,' Imogen answered. 'It's helped in a way. I know I've had enough of it. I know the money's going to be less—I'm at the bottom rung in midwifery and at the top in Emergency, but some things are just more important. I'm going to apply for a full-time job in maternity.'

'You might change your mind.'

'I already told you, Angus, I *don't* change my mind.'

She was telling him something and it hurt to hear it— any relief he'd felt earlier that she wasn't with Brad countered by the agony of the future she was mapping out without him.

'Look Imogen...' It was Angus's turn now to open up. 'I haven't been completely honest with you.'

'Did you sleep with Gemma?' There, she had been brave enough to say it, a few years older and brave enough to confront what she hadn't been able to a few years ago.

'Why do you always do that, Imogen?' Angus asked. 'Why do you have to dash to the worst-case scenario all the time?'

'Because it usually is.'

'Was,' Angus said gently. 'Imogen, it's over between me and Gemma. Even my mum's starting to believe it. We went out for lunch last week, but that was more to see if we could handle the divorce without lawyers.'

'Can you?'

'Nope!' Angus gave a half-grin.

'So when weren't you honest?'

'When I said why I didn't want anyone at work to know.' He blew out a breath, and she knew it was a long one because the freezing night made it white and it went on for ever. 'Everything I said, I meant—I mean, I did feel uncomfortable about people knowing, especially given how soon after Gemma it happened and how long you'd be here, especially that you were leaving… But that wasn't entirely the reason…'

'Just say it Angus.' Her eyes brimmed with tears that she hoped he couldn't see.

'I didn't want Heather to know. I felt it would be unfair to her.'

'Heather?' Imogen did a double-take.

'I'm trusting you with this…'

'You and Heather?' She saw him frown. 'I'm sorry—of course you can trust me not to say anything.'

'She's got a bit of a thing for me…' He said it only with kindness. 'She had too much to drink at one of the work Christmas parties a couple of years ago and out it came. Nothing happened, of course,' Angus said, and she was grateful she had bitten her tongue to refrain from asking. 'And I told her nothing ever would happen, you know, that I was flattered and everything, but that I was happily married… She was mortified the next day—rang me in tears, even offered to resign, but look…' He gave an uncomfortable shrug. 'I sort of pretended that I'd had too much to drink and couldn't really remember all she'd said. It made it easier for her…' And that he would do that for Heather made her eyes fill with tears for entirely different reasons.

This, one of the many reasons she loved about him. Loved him.

Which was why she'd shown him all of her—or most of her.

'I just think it would be a bit of a kick in the teeth for her,' Angus explained further. 'She's rung a couple of times, I've tried to put her off.'

'Maybe she just wants to be friends now.'

'She is a friend.' Angus nodded. 'Which is why I don't want to hurt her.

'Imogen…' She knew what was coming, knew what he was going to ask, knew he wanted the rest of her that she was so very scared to give. 'Why do you think I don't want people to know?'

'Because it's too soon…' she attempted.

'Why else?' Holding her hands, even if he wasn't looking at her, Imogen knew that he'd seen her, not just here and now and not just naked, but that he could see inside her very soul, see the bits she thought she had long ago dealt with and never wanted to show again. And the bits she'd sworn she'd never let another man see.

'Brad was embarrassed to be seen with me.'

'Then he's a fool.'

'Look at Gemma and look at me…'

'I'm not comparing.'

'Of course you are.' Imogen snapped. 'I do! I look at Brad and I look at you and you're both good-looking, all the women adore you, you're both on television—'

'How's this for a comparison, then,' Angus broke

in. 'We're both crazy about you and while Brad, I'm sure, is regretting losing you, I know that I'm about to face the same…'

'Then do something about it.'

'Like what?' Angus asked, only there wasn't an answer. 'I hated geography at school,' Angus said. 'Now I know why.'

She didn't smile at his joke and neither did he—just stood in endless silence, wanting the agony over but never wanting it to end. 'A couple more minutes…' he glanced at his watch and tried to lighten things up. 'Hey, it's already New Year's Day for you! What's the time difference in Australia?'

'No, it's New Year's Eve for me too,' Imogen corrected him, her voice utterly steady, her eyes holding his as she conveyed the seriousness of her words, 'because everything I love most in the world is here, right now, in London.'

It could never be wrong to kiss her.

Even if it could never last, never work, even if in a few days she'd be gone, it could never be wrong to kiss her, and it would never be pointless to prolong it.

Because pulling her into his arms, feeling the sweet taste of her as he parted her lips with his tongue, every second, every minute that he kissed her, held her, adored her was another minute he could remember for ever.

'Hey…' Ever the chameleon, she pulled back just a fraction, their warm breaths mingling. 'If you make love to me here, at least we won't have to say we haven't had sex this year…'

'As much as I might want to…' Angus grinned even

though his eyes were glassy '…I am not going to have sex on the fire escape at work!'

'Spoilsport,' she teased.

'Imogen…' He kissed her again, but was adamant. 'It's a measure of how much I love you that I'm not going to.' He stopped then, stopped because he'd never meant to say it, had never really let himself feel it. Love wasn't supposed to come along just yet.

Love was something in the distance, something that would maybe happen in his life later, much later, but love was what it was, right here, right now, and he was holding it in his arms.

'I love you, Imogen.'

Only she didn't say it back. Instead, she stared back at him for the longest time, then blinked a few times before she gave her strange answer and turned to go.

'Then you'd *really* better do something about it.'

'How were the fireworks?' Heather asked as they returned to the still quiet department.

'Spectacular.' Imogen grinned, picking up a fruit kebab and making Angus's stomach fold over on itself as she licked the tip of a strawberry. Then she added for Angus's benefit, 'But they fizzled out at the end—not quite the big bang I was hoping for!'

'Could you hurry up and see her, please?' Heather said as she handed Angus a chart. 'The husband's getting a bit worked up.'

'Sorry?' Angus frowned.

'Louise Williams, the abdo pain in cubicle four. Oh, sorry.' She gave an apologetic smile. 'It was Gus I spoke to about her—she's twenty weeks pregnant, had a miscarriage earlier in the year, oh, it's last year now…'

And Imogen saw it then.

Saw how often Heather called for Angus if there was a problem, how Heather arranged her breaks around his and probably her shifts too—and saw how hard it would be, not just for Angus but for Heather too, if the truth came out.

Not that she had time to dwell on it, not when at fifteen minutes past midnight on New Years Day the fireworks went off again.

CHAPTER FIFTEEN

'WE'VE GOT multiple stabbings coming in.' Heather had to practically shout as a group of young men spilled out of the waiting room, security men quickly onto them as the waiting room started to fill. 'Gus is onto it and the surgeons are coming. Imogen,' she called out, 'can you take the abdo pain?'

The noises in the department did nothing to soothe the terrified woman and Imogen held her hand as Angus gently probed her abdomen, Louise's anxious husband hovering.

'You've had no bleeding?' Angus checked.

'None. Just this pain. I'm losing my baby, aren't I?'

'Let me take a look at you,' Angus said firmly, 'before we rush to any conclusions. Now, have you had any nausea or vomiting?'

'I feel sick,' Louise said, 'but I haven't been sick.'

'How's your appetite?'

'I can't eat.'

'OK…' Angus checked the card which had her observations recorded. 'I'm just going to get the Doppler.'

'Doppler?' Louise's eyes darted to Imogen.

'It's just a little machine, so he can listen to the baby's heartbeat.'

'Oh, God!'

'Just try and take it easy,' Imogen said gently, but even though she was calm and reassuring, Imogen did let out a breath when, after only a few seconds of trying to locate it, the delicious sounds of a strong, regular foetal heartbeat was picked up.

'OK…' Angus gave a thin smile at the heartbeat. 'That's certainly good news. You're a bit dehydrated. I see Heather put in a drip and took some bloods—I'm going to get those sent straight to the lab and I'm going to get some IV fluids started on you…'

'Aren't you going to examine me?' Louise flushed. 'I mean…'

'I'm not going to do a PV,' Angus said, 'because the obstetrician is going to want to do one and if your uterus is a bit irritable, I don't want to disturb things. I'm just going to speak with a colleague and then I'll come back and talk to you.'

'What do you think is wrong?'

'Let me just have a quick word with the surgeon and then I'll be back.'

'The surgeon!' Louise startled, but Angus was already gone, leaving Imogen to deal with a less than impressed husband.

'What?' he demanded. 'Are we too menial to even be told what he's thinking?'

'We've got a surgical emergency in Resus,' Imogen said calmly. 'I suspect he wants to catch the team before they race off to Theatre.'

'Oh.'

Which was exactly the case, as it turned out. The surgical consultant made a brief appearance and examined Louise, then went outside the cubicle to talk to Angus as the couple became more agitated. Once Louise had been for an urgent ultrasound, Imogen did her observations regularly and tried to reassure them, only she was practically running between patients as the waiting room filled fit to burst, nurses, doctors everywhere calling out for assistance. If they'd had double the staff on tonight, it still wouldn't have been enough.

'Will someone please have the decency to tell us what the hell is going on!'

Imogen, wearing gloves and holding up an inebriated patient's tea towel–wrapped hand that contained a partially severed finger wasn't really in a position to calm the furious Mr Williams as he stormed out of the cubicle. 'My wife's in bloody agony and all you lot keep saying is that you're waiting for blood results.'

'The obstetrician's on his way down,' Imogen said, 'just as soon—'

'I don't want to hear how busy he is!' Mr Williams roared, coming up to her, shouting right in her face. 'I don't want to know about other patients, when my wife…'

As his voice trailed off Imogen actually thought he was going to hit her, could do nothing to defend herself as she held on to her patient. She could see the hairs up his nose and the veins bulging in his forehead, could hear her patient slurring obscenities in her defence, and then she realized that he *was* going to hit her. She could see his fist, and behind that Angus dropping the phone and racing over, but Security got there first, grabbing his hand before it made contact, coming between the relative and the nurse, taking control of the situation, as they often did.

It was a non-event really—something that happened, something she was more than used to dealing with. She was just utterly weary to the bone of being *used* to dealing with it.

'I'll take him for you.'

Cassie saw Imogen's pale face and relieved her of her drunken patient as Imogen peeled off her bloodied gloves while Angus read the Riot Act.

'If you ever threaten or verbally abuse my staff again I will have you removed from the department and arrested!' There was no doubt from his voice that he meant every word.

'I didn't threaten her!'

Even though Angus was completely in control, his anger was palpable, contempt lacing every word as he responded to Mr Williams.

'When a six-foot man gets in the face of a woman and shouts, believe me, sir, it's extremely threatening. And when that same man raises his fist…'

'I wasn't going to hit her!'

Debatable perhaps—only there simply wasn't time.

'Now…' Angus let out a long breath. 'Even though it seems you have been here ages, it has, in fact, been an hour. In that time your wife has been examined by myself and the surgeon, she has had an IV started and bloods taken and has been sent for an ultrasound. I was actually on the phone just now getting some results and was about to come in and talk to you.'

'Hi, there.' Whistling as he walked, grinning as he came over, Oliver Hanson, incredibly laid-back, dressed in theatre scrubs and oblivious to all that had occurred, joined the little gathering. 'Hi, there, Imogen—good to see you.' Then he raised his eyebrows to Angus. 'I hear you've got a suspected appendicitis for me to see— twenty weeks gestation.'

Which wasn't the best way to deliver the potential diagnosis, but then the whole exercise had been a bit of a disaster. A touch pale in the face and a bit grim-lipped, Imogen followed the doctors and Mr Williams into the cubicle as Security hovered outside.

'I'm sorry!' Mr Williams glanced over at Imogen, who nodded.

'He didn't mean to scare you.' Louise was in tears. 'He's just worried about me.'

'Let's listen to the doctors.' Imogen forced a smile, told herself that it wasn't Louise's fault she was married to this man. It was simply her job to put the patient at ease, only it was getting harder and harder to do.

'We think you have appendicitis,' Angus started. 'It's difficult to diagnose in pregnancy as there are some tests we can't do because they may affect the baby. Some of the changes in blood that happen during pregnancy make the lab findings more difficult to interpret too. The ultrasound of your abdomen appears normal, which has ruled out some other tentative diagnoses and I've spoken again to Mr Lucas, the surgeon who saw you, and he agrees that appendicitis is the most likely diagnosis. However, until you have the operation, we won't know for sure.'

'But isn't that dangerous for the baby?'

'It's far more dangerous for the baby if your appendix ruptures,' Oliver explained. 'That's why we'd prefer not to wait. Yes, there is a chance that the surgery might cause premature labour, but I'll start an infusion that should hopefully prevent that, and we'll work closely with the anaesthetist. We all want your pregnancy to continue.'

'So there's no real choice?' Mr Williams's voice was gruff.

'No.' Angus spoke to his patient. 'Mr Lucas is in Theatre and he'll be ready for you soon, so the best thing we can do is get you up as quickly as possible. You've had some IV fluids so you're better hydrated now and the anaesthetist is going to come down and talk to you but, yes, we'll get you up as soon as possible.'

'You'll be OK.' Imogen smiled once all the doctors had gone and she prepared Louise for Theatre, collecting all her notes and going through the endless check lists.

'I never even thought it could be appendicitis—I thought I was losing the baby.'

'It's always your first thought when you're pregnant, but appendicitis is just as common during pregnancy as it is at other times—just more complicated. You'll go up to Maternity after the operation so they can watch the baby closely.'

'You've seen this before then?'

'I'm a midwife.' Imogen nodded. 'So, yes, I've seen it before.'

'A midwife?' Louise frowned. 'So what are you do-ing working here?'

'Earning a living.' Imogen answered, as the porter clicked off the brakes on the trolley and they headed through the bedlam of the emergency department, tears stinging her eyes as she gave the wrong but honest answer.

'You've been marvellous as always, Imogen!' Always generous with praise for her staff, Heather thanked Imogen profusely as she signed her time sheet at seven-thirty a.m. The place was still full, patients everywhere, linen skips and bins overflowing, but order was slowly being restored. 'Have a look at the roster before you go and take your pick—there are plenty of shifts to be filled this week.'

'No, thanks!' Pulling off her hair-tie, Imogen hoisted her bag on her shoulder. 'I'm done.'

'I thought you were here for a little while longer?'

'I mean with Emergency.' Oh, so casually she'd said it, but Heather quickly noticed the wobble in her voice. 'I'm calling it a day.'

'Imogen!' Heather's voice was full of concern, caus-ing a few nurses to turn round. 'Did that incident with Mr Williams—?'

'I'd made up my mind before that,' Imogen inter-rupted. 'I'm just…' she gave a helpless shrug '…tired of it, I guess. Burnt out—isn't that what they say? I love Emergency and everything. It's just getting too much, since I had Heath.'

'Excuse me!' Looking nothing like the angry, rag-ing man from earlier, Mr Williams appeared at the nurses' station. 'Louise had her operation and the baby seems fine.'

'That's good to know,' Imogen said, and the smile she gave was genuine because it *was* good to know.

'About before.' He was red in the face again, but for different reasons this time. 'I really am sorry for what happened.'

His apology was genuine, Imogen knew that.

And she was about to open her mouth, to tell him it was OK, that he had been stressed and worried about his wife and the baby and that it didn't matter.

Only it did.

It mattered a lot.

Mr Williams wasn't the reason she was giving up a job she loved, but the Mr Williamses of the world were a big part of it.

And somehow sorry wasn't enough for Imogen this morning.

His apology, no matter how genuine, just one she couldn't accept any more. Without a word she walked off and left him standing there, tears streaming down her face as she exited through the ambulance bay, before finally she said the words she'd really wanted to.

'So you should be!'

CHAPTER SIXTEEN

SHE so did not need this.

Stamping through the slush, Imogen wished she'd been more assertive, wished she'd just stuck to her guns and refused to take the shift.

OK, they'd assured her that she wouldn't actually be in Emergency, that the nurse unit manager had agreed that she could stay in the observation ward. Only that made it worse somehow—being there and not doing anything, hearing the buzz of Emergency and not being a part of it.

Seeing Angus again.

The only thing worse than that was the thought of *not* seeing him again.

It had been four days since they'd last kissed, four days since she'd, cryptically perhaps, laid her heart on the line and four days when he hadn't done a thing about it.

No phone call.

No text.

Nothing.

So what if he'd said he loved her? For all he knew she could be on a plane already winging her way back to Queensland with Heath, which was probably what he wanted, Imogen thought, her face stinging as the heat of the hospital hit her frozen cheeks. Yes, once she was safely out the country there would be no chance of their embarrassing little interlude coming out, no explanations necessary.

The heat had nothing to do with the tears that suddenly pricked her eyes.

'Hi, Imogen…' Cassie greeted her warmly. 'Go and grab a coffee before handover.'

'I'm in Obs.' Imogen forced a smile. 'I'll just head straight round there.'

'You've got time for a coffee,' Cassie insisted. 'Actually, I'll join you. I never got my break this morning, the place was bedlam as usual…' She chatted away as they walked, two nurses heading off to the staffroom. Cassie could never have known how much it hurt Imogen to glimpse Resus, see the machines, the patients, the buzz of Emergency that she loved but which didn't love her back, that just hurt too much to stay.

She actually wanted to turn and run—she could turn and run. She was an agency nurse, easily replaced, could plead a migraine, anything, as long as she didn't have to put herself through it.

'Surprise!'

Opening the staffroom door, it really was one.

Colleagues and friends she had only just made all standing there to greet her, the table laid with Chinese take-aways and cola and crisps. Emergency staff only ever needed a teeny excuse to throw a party, but that they might throw one for her—an agency nurse who had done just a very few shifts—was unfathomable.

'Now…' Heather handed her a cup of cola and took the floor. 'We don't do this for everyone, but we're not losing an agency nurse—the nursing world's losing a good emergency nurse and we figured she deserved a bit of a send-off! How long have you been one of us?'

'Ten years?' Imogen gulped.

'Then you've more than earned a party.'

They'd signed a card and her eyes blurred as she read the messages, especially Angus's. Short and sweet, he'd wished her luck in her new career, thanked her for her hard work here and signed it without love, and with very best wishes for her future—just not theirs.

Which was to be expected, of course.

It just hurt.

Hurt too that he couldn't make it, Heather explained, because he was recording his TV show.

And when the party was over, sitting in the obs ward, her one head injury patient snoring his head off, Imogen knew that ten cardiac arrests and a few stabbings would be much easier to deal with than her own thoughts.

Sitting in a busy department in a busy city, never had she felt more alone.

'Why don't you have your break?' Heather bustled round. 'I'll watch Mr Knight.'

'I've been sitting down for three hours!' Imogen pulled her head out of the book she was desperately trying to concentrate on. 'I don't need a break.'

'Well, I do!' Heather said, sliding into the seat beside her. 'I really am glad you came in today.'

'I am too. It was really thoughtful of you all...' Imogen flushed. 'I wasn't expecting it.'

'Not just for that. That incident with Mr Williams...I didn't want you leaving on a bad note...'

'He's not the reason I'm finishing up.'

'I know that, but it did upset you.'

'It didn't used to,' Imogen explained. 'I used to be able to shrug it off. I just can't any more. So now it's either get upset or get hard and cynical—and I don't want that to be me.'

'That isn't you,' Heather agreed. 'I do know how you feel, after the week we've had here, what with Maria Vanaldi and everything...'

'Maria?'

'You haven't seen the news?'

'They don't have televisions in the rooms at the youth hostel—what about Maria?'

'It wasn't an accident.'

'The car lost control...'

'It had been tampered with. It was her husband's family apparently.'

And Imogen closed her eyes, knowing in that moment that the choice she'd struggled so hard to come to had, for her, been the right one.

'Go and have your break,' Heather said again, and this time Imogen didn't refuse.

His voice in the room hurt.

Imogen was glad that even though she'd joked with Maria about it, she'd never actually thought to record

Angus's show because, seeing him, hearing him and not being able to have him hurt in a way it didn't when she watched Brad.

She knew that if she did have a recording, she'd torture herself over and over, watching his beautiful, proud face, slightly defiant as the carefully scripted interview commenced.

She put more bread in the toaster and stood in the empty staffroom, tears streaming down her face as she rammed the lovely buttery toast into her mouth and waited for the next round to toast, wishing it would fill the hole in her soul. She listened as they spoke about viewers who were lonely and ill over Christmas, listened as they talked about the miracle that should be Christmas but in reality how incredibly hard it was for some people at this time of year.

And then came the difficult part.

Imogen could hear the shift in tone from the interviewer and watched Angus's chin lift a fraction, ready to face the public music. Only it wasn't quite the tune she was expecting to hear.

'A lot of our viewers are going to be sorry to hear that this is to be your final regular appearance on the show.'

'That's correct.' Angus nodded.

'We've seen in the newspapers this week—' his colleague, no doubt his friend, cleared her throat just a touch '—that your own marriage just ended.'

'It did.' And because he was a so-called celebrity, because part of his job was asking people to bare their lives, Imogen screwed her eyes closed as Angus, this private, beautiful man, was forced to open up—if not for the good of himself, then for the good of all.

'Did that have any impact on your decision to leave the show?'

'Of course,' Angus answered brusquely, and Imogen could only smile at his closed-off expression, the same one she'd seen when they'd sat in the café that first time together.

'It must be a painful time.'

'It's a…' There was a pause, just a beat of a pause that had her open her eyes, that had the interviewer frowning just a touch, as maybe, just maybe, Angus deviated from the script. 'It's a *searching* time,' he said carefully, but on behalf of so many, so, so eloquently he added, 'For all involved.'

'It's been reported that there was another party involved—do you have any comment you'd like to make to that?'

And she went to bite into her toast but changed her mind, her throat so thick with tears that there wasn't room for anything else. She waited for his polite rebuttal, for his clipped 'No comment', for his request for his family's privacy—only it never came.

'My wife, without malice or intent, fell in love with someone else.'

'Oh!' Imogen saw the slight, frantic dart of the interviewer's eyes. She smiled, despite her tears, as with candour, honesty and integrity he reached into living rooms everywhere and showed the world a little bit of why he really was so special.

'And you don't fall in love with someone else if things are good at home,' Angus continued, borrowing Imogen's script for a moment then reverting back to his own. 'And for that I take my full share of the responsibility.'

'That's very forgiving.'

'You don't choose with whom, when and where you fall in love,' Angus responded coolly. 'I didn't understand that, but now, thanks to a very special person, I do.'

'So…' The interviewer was shuffling her papers now, staring at them as if willing something to leap out and tell her what the hell to say. 'You're saying that you too—'

'Absolutely.' Imogen's gasp came as the staffroom door opened, knew without turning it was him, could feel his arms wrap around her as he held her from behind and stared at her from the screen. 'There is the most wonderful woman in my life at the moment and I intend to keep it that way. I'm going to learn from my mistakes, which,' he added, 'we actually do all make.

'Gemma and I decided to be honest.' His words were soft and low in her ear. 'She doesn't deserve to be portrayed as the guilty party in this. We both just want it over, so we decided to be upfront and just get it all over and done with. Gemma has my support, even if it nearly killed me to give it on national television…'

'I'm so proud of you.'

'I'm proud of me too,' Angus said. 'And I'm proud of you too.'

'For what?'

'For being you. For making me see.' And he didn't add '*sense*' or '*things more clearly*.' He didn't need to, because his eyes were open. Now he really could see that there was so much more than two sides to a story, that the two sides had other sides, and those other sides had other sides too. People were people and that was OK. That was what made them real.

'You didn't call me.'

'I didn't know what to say,' Angus admitted. 'I knew I had to offer you something, only I didn't know what. And then things got busy… Maria Vanaldi…'

'I heard it wasn't an accident.'

'It got nasty—the police contacted me to ask if Maria had said anything, and I went round to see Ainslie. I was worried about her being caught up in it all and not knowing what was going on. I spoke to Elijah…'

'Guido's uncle?'

'He's his guardian now. And that sounds simple, only this man lives in Italy, a rich playboy who hops on planes the way we take the underground and he didn't even know if he wanted to do it—and then he fell in love with his nephew. A few days with Guido and he's turning his life around if it means that he can keep him.'

And that Guido was safe, that he would be loved and looked after was the nicest thing she could have hoped to hear, or, Imogen admitted, gazing into jade eyes that adored her, almost the nicest.

'You were never the easy option,' he said, turning her to face him. 'You were never a quick fling or convenient or not good enough or any one of those things you beat yourself up with. You were the most difficult option possible, Imogen.'

'Why?'

'Because you live on the other side of the world,

because in a few days you'll be back there with your Heath and I'll be here with Clemmie and Jack. You were absolutely the last person it made sense to fall in love with.' He pulled up her chin to make her look at him. 'You were never a threat to my marriage—it was over long before you came along. The only threat you were was to my sanity. The craziest thing I could do was fall in love with you, but I did. I love you. I absolutely love you. And I don't know how, but I know it can work.' She opened her mouth to talk, but it was Angus's turn still. 'I can't bear the thought of you on the other side of the world without me there beside you every day, but it's a far better option than losing you. I don't care if people say long-distance love can't work, because those people don't know me and they don't know you...

'I don't change my mind either and I won't change my mind about this. If I have to spend every minute of annual leave flying to see you, if I have to work every shift I can so I can fly you back to see me just as much as you can, if we can't properly be together till the kids are much older—we'll still be together, if only you'll have me.'

That he would give her his heart, and let her go with it, that he trusted her enough to return with it whenever she could was the greatest gift of them all—a miracle really, Imogen thought, smiling through her tears as he kissed her swollen buttery mouth till it was she who pulled away.

'It's a Christmas miracle!'

'It is...' Angus grumbled, not caring that Heather had just walked in, not dropping Imogen or pulling back, just wanting to kiss and taste her again, because she was his—she really was.

'No…' Imogen gave a giggle. 'Shane's going into remission.'

'Shane?'

'Shane!'

'But he's only got two weeks to live!' Heather's shocked gasp had Imogen giggling. Heather loved the show—loved, loved, loved it, taped every episode and was always pumping Imogen for inside info. 'It's completely incurable—Dr Adams said so last night.'

'It's a miracle, I tell you!' Imogen said, waving her hands like a gospel singer, then as Angus watched on, bemused, the two women doubled over in a fit of laughing.

'Don't breathe a word!' Imogen warned. 'If the story line ever gets out…'

'Praise be!' Heather said, grinning, slipping out and, unbeknown to them standing guard on the other side of the door so that no one could possibly disturb them.

'She knows?' Imogen checked.

'I told her.'

'So the party…'

'The party was their idea. Heather just told me that you'd be back today. Imogen, when did you find out about Brad?' Puzzled eyes frowned down at her. 'Is that what you two had to discuss?'

'Brad and I had to talk.' She was suddenly serious and always, always beautiful. 'He's been offered another year's work here and he wants to take it.'

'And you couldn't tell me that?' He didn't get it.

'Imogen, have you any idea what I've been through, trying to think of ways we could be together, trying to come up with a solution? And all the while you had one.'

'I had a temporary solution, Angus, and we both deserve a lot more than that. Brad just dropped it on me—his character proved popular and they offered him a year's contract. Of course, my first instinct was to say yes, but it wasn't a solution. What happens in a year when his contract's up, what happens if I hate it here? And why should I leave a home and family I love because Brad's been offered a job? If you and Gemma got back together or if you and I didn't work out, I needed to be sure I was staying for the right reasons...'

And he got it then, got what a huge decision it must have been for her. 'It took a glass or two of wine and a lot of tears but we actually managed some very grown-up talking—something neither of us are very good at. He had to get it that I can't just follow my ex-husband around the globe, and I had to get my head around the fact that you couldn't come into my decision either.' She saw him frown. 'This had to be about Heath and I.' She took a big breath. 'Whether I could stand to be in London without you.'

'Could you?'

'I can stand anything, Angus.' She gave him her soft smile. 'But I'd rather do it with you.'

'Then you will.'

'But what about next year...when his contract...?'

'Who knows?' Angus hushed her with his lips. 'This, I do know, though, we'll work it out.'

'Will we?' And he saw her blink a couple of times, just as he had that first day. He saw again that this soft, utterly together woman sometimes got nervous, sometimes got scared, and it thrilled him that he could read her, could comfort her and could love her.

'Always!'

'I FEEL so fat!'

Angus looked over to where Imogen lay.

'I could think of so many better ways to describe you.'

Oh, and he could.

Dressed in her favourite red bikini, they'd been enjoying a gentle dip in the pool after a massive Christmas barbecue and now Imogen was on the lounger, her belly ripe with their baby, her skin freckled by the hot Queensland sun. It was still as if each day the colour in his world brightened.

What could potentially have been the worst year of his life had been the best.

Clemmie and Jack thriving, as their parents did the same.

Thanks to Imogen.

Thanks to this funny, complicated, beautiful woman who had stepped into the path of an oncoming train and somehow made them all change track.

Christmas in Australia!

Who'd have thought?

Hauling himself out of the pool and lying on the

lounger next to her, dripping water as he went, Angus watched the three kids splashing and playing in the water, then grinned over to where Imogen lay. 'They're having a ball.'

'They're killing me,' Imogen groaned. 'They've been up since five!'

'It's been a long day, having all your family over and everything, but we can go to bed soon,' Angus pointed out. 'Brad will be here soon and Gemma and Roger just texted to say they were on their way.'

'Good!'

Who'd have thought?

Angus lay back as Imogen heaved herself up again and then joined the kids in the pool for one last play before they headed off to enjoy the rest of Christmas Day with their other families.

She'd wanted to have their baby in Australia.

Which should have been impossible as they'd all wanted Christmas with the children.

But because, through it all, Imogen had been consistently nice and kind and infinitely understanding, somehow that sentiment grew and somehow, when needed, the universe gave back.

Taking some long overdue leave, Angus was even doing the odd stint in Australia, realising in years to come he might well do many shifts more. The home she'd struggled so hard to keep for Heath was now a furnished rental that the hospital used, only not these past weeks. Tentative plans put forward had been made so much easier when Gemma and Roger had decided that bringing the children for a holiday in Australia might be rather nice. Brad too had taken time off from his very busy schedule and was even planning to negotiate four weeks off each Christmas.

Impossible almost, yet they'd worked it out.

For Imogen.

He was quite a nice guy really, Angus conceded as, sunglasses on, long hair so blond it was white now, Brad sauntered into the back yard and the kids leapt out of the pool to greet him.

Yes, quite a nice guy for a thickhead, Angus thought as Brad knelt down and kissed Imogen on the cheek.

Oh, his solar plexus still got the odd workout, but nothing too major. And a bit of jealously was OK, Imogen had pointed out, if it kept him on his elbows!

'Hey, Angus!'

'Merry Christmas, Brad,' Angus responded, just a touch formally.

'Do you want me to watch them?'

'Watch them?' Angus could see his frown in the mirrored sunglasses.

'Till Gemma gets here.' He nodded in Imogen's direction and Angus was on his feet in an instant. Her forearms were resting on the edge of the pool, a look of intense concentration on her face. Suddenly Brad wasn't the thickhead here, because a doctor and a midwife they may be, but it had taken the actor to first realise what was happening. Irritable, restless, Imogen wasn't tired and cranky—she was in labour.

Imogen had worked it out, though, by the time he got poolside.

'I wanted a water birth...' Imogen stopped talking

then, her face bright red and screwed up in agony for a long moment till finally she blew out. 'But I'm not having it in the pool!'

'Heath took for ever,' Brad drawled, 'but doesn't the second one usually come quicker? At least, that's what you used to say…'

'Thanks, Brad!' Angus snapped. 'Just watch the kids, bring the car round…'

'Just get me into the house,' Imogen groaned through gritted teeth. 'Brad, call an ambulance.'

This was so not how she'd planned it. A full-time midwife practically till the moment they'd flown back to Australia, she'd worked out her birth plan, and being hauled up the pools steps and led to the house, her ex-husband the one ringing for an ambulance and watching the kids as Angus steered her inside, wasn't a part of it.

'Let's get to the bedroom.' Angus was trying to be calm, but Imogen could hear the note of panic in his voice and it panicked her. Nothing fazed Angus, nothing medical anyway.

'The bathroom…' Imogen gasped. 'I don't want to ruin my silk bedspread…'

'Never mind the bloody bedspread.'

'But I broke the snow globe.'

The silk bedspread wasn't ever going to be an issue, the living-room floor having to suffice, Angus sweating despite the air conditioner on full blast as he pulled off her bikini bottoms.

'I wanted drugs.'

'I know.'

'I wanted to go in the spa.'

'I know…' Angus gritted his teeth. 'Just try and breathe through it. The ambulance will be here soon.'

'Angus…' As another contraction hit and she just really, really had to push, she also really had to ask. 'There's something wrong.'

'There's nothing wrong.' Angus tried to steady himself, attempted a reassuring smile. 'It's got red hair!'

'Poor thing.' Imogen tried to smile back but started crying, because she could see the panic in his eyes, see the grim set of his jaw, knew that he was seriously worried. 'I've worked alongside you—I know when something's going wrong.'

'Nothing's going wrong,' Angus said, only it didn't soothe her. 'It's just never been you before.' And in her panic it didn't make sense, but in that moment between contractions, that last moment between birth and born, the mist cleared.

He loved her.

Absolutely loved her.

And love made things a bit scary sometimes because the stakes were so high.

'It's all good.' Angus said. 'All looks completely normal.'

And it was.

Scary but good. Agony sometimes, but completely and utterly healthy and normal—this thing called living.

Imogen got to deliver her herself, with a bit of help from Angus, lifting their daughter out together and watching in awe as blue eyes opened and she screamed her welcome. A blaze of red, from kicking feet and fists that punched in rage, right to her little screwed-up face and tufts of red hair.

'She's perfect…'

'She is,' Angus said, because it was all he could manage, actually relieved when the paramedics arrived and he could just be a dad.

'Born under a Christmas tree,' the paramedic greeted them. 'You're going to have some fun picking names.'

'Do I have to go to hospital?'

'You need to be checked,' the paramedic said. 'The little one too.'

'You can have that spa,' Angus said temptingly when her face fell. 'And champagne and…' He grinned. 'I can ask Gemma if she minds cleaning up the mess!'

And they were the nicest paramedics, Angus thought, high on adrenaline and loving everyone. They were in absolutely no rush, even happy to let her freshen up a bit once they'd got her on the stretcher and Imogen had decided that she really didn't want Gemma to see her coming out looking quite this bad!

'I want Heath.'

So Angus got him. His usually happy face, pinched and worried, but relaxing into a smile when he saw his new sister. Jack looked pretty chuffed too and Clemmie burst into tears because she'd desperately wanted a boy so that she'd still be the only girl. And then Heath looking worried again when it really was time to get them to the hospital.

'He'll be OK.' Brad assured them, and Angus had to swallow, not jealousy now, maybe even a tear as he saw a slightly wistful look on Brad's face as he gave Imogen a fond kiss goodbye. 'I'll bring him up to see you later tonight.' He looked over at Angus. 'If that's OK with you guys.'

'That'd be great.'

'Us too?' Clemmie asked.

'Yes, you too!' Gemma smiled but her eyes were a little bit glassy, a wistful look on her face as for the first time she met Imogen's eyes. 'Congratulations!'

'Congratulations!' Brad shook Angus's hand and Roger did the same.

Yep, just a bit painful sometimes, Imogen thought as they wheeled her off—for all concerned—but worth it.

And what better way to spend Christmas night? Tucked up in bed, champagne in hand, choosing from a massive chocolate selection with Angus cuddled up beside her, choosing names for a certain little lady who didn't have one yet.

'Holly?' Imogen said again.

'Natalie?' Angus frowned. 'You know, there really aren't that many to choose from.'

'I know!' Imogen breathed, staring over to her daughter, her hair all fluffy after her first bath, her complexion creamy now, fair eyelashes curling upwards, her little snub nose covered by her hand as she sucked on her thumb.

'Summer!'

'Summer?' Angus creased up his nose. 'That's not a Christmas name.'

'She was born in summer.'

'But Christmas is in winter in England, it won't make sense.'

'It will to us.'

'A December baby called Summer!' Angus looked over to his sleeping new daughter. A little ray of sunshine, a little bit of summer, no matter how cold the winter, and, yes, he conceded happily, Imogen was right and he kissed her to tell her so.

'Summer Lake…' Imogen sighed, coming up for breath.

'Summer Maitlin,' Angus corrected, kissing her again.

'Summer Lake-Maitlin.' Imogen said, and then she smiled. 'We'll keep working on it.'

MILLS & BOON®
Pure reading pleasure™

OCTOBER 2008 HARDBACK TITLES

ROMANCE

The Greek Tycoon's Disobedient Bride	978 0 263 20366 0
Lynne Graham	
The Venetian's Midnight Mistress	978 0 263 20367 7
Carole Mortimer	
Ruthless Tycoon, Innocent Wife *Helen Brooks*	978 0 263 20368 4
The Sheikh's Wayward Wife *Sandra Marton*	978 0 263 20369 1
The Fiorenza Forced Marriage *Melanie Milburne*	978 0 263 20370 7
The Spanish Billionaire's Christmas Bride	978 0 263 20371 4
Maggie Cox	
The Ruthless Italian's Inexperienced Wife	978 0 263 20372 1
Christina Hollis	
Claimed for the Italian's Revenge *Natalie Rivers*	978 0 263 20373 8
The Italian's Christmas Miracle *Lucy Gordon*	978 0 263 20374 5
Cinderella and the Cowboy *Judy Christenberry*	978 0 263 20375 2
His Mistletoe Bride *Cara Colter*	978 0 263 20376 9
Pregnant: Father Wanted *Claire Baxter*	978 0 263 20377 6
Marry-Me Christmas *Shirley Jump*	978 0 263 20378 3
Her Baby's First Christmas *Susan Meier*	978 0 263 20379 0
One Magical Christmas *Carol Marinelli*	978 0 263 20380 6
The GP's Meant-To-Be Bride *Jennifer Taylor*	978 0 263 20381 3

HISTORICAL

Miss Winbolt and the Fortune Hunter	978 0 263 20213 7
Sylvia Andrew	
Captain Fawley's Innocent Bride *Annie Burrows*	978 0 263 20214 4
The Rake's Rebellious Lady *Anne Herries*	978 0 263 20215 1

MEDICAL™

A Mummy for Christmas *Caroline Anderson*	978 0 263 19914 7
A Bride and Child Worth Waiting For	978 0 263 19915 4
Marion Lennox	
The Italian Surgeon's Christmas Miracle	978 0 263 19916 1
Alison Roberts	
Children's Doctor, Christmas Bride *Lucy Clark*	978 0 263 19917 8

OCTOBER 2008 LARGE PRINT TITLES

ROMANCE

The Sheikh's Blackmailed Mistress *Penny Jordan*	978 0 263 20082 9
The Millionaire's Inexperienced Love-Slave *Miranda Lee*	978 0 263 20083 6
Bought: The Greek's Innocent Virgin *Sarah Morgan*	978 0 263 20084 3
Bedded at the Billionaire's Convenience *Cathy Williams*	978 0 263 20085 0
The Pregnancy Promise *Barbara McMahon*	978 0 263 20086 7
The Italian's Cinderella Bride *Lucy Gordon*	978 0 263 20087 4
Saying Yes to the Millionaire *Fiona Harper*	978 0 263 20088 1
Her Royal Wedding Wish *Cara Colter*	978 0 263 20089 8

HISTORICAL

Untouched Mistress *Margaret McPhee*	978 0 263 20169 7
A Less Than Perfect Lady *Elizabeth Beacon*	978 0 263 20170 3
Viking Warrior, Unwilling Wife *Michelle Styles*	978 0 263 20171 0

MEDICAL™

The Doctor's Royal Love-Child *Kate Hardy*	978 0 263 19980 2
His Island Bride *Marion Lennox*	978 0 263 19981 9
A Consultant Beyond Compare *Joanna Neil*	978 0 263 19982 6
The Surgeon Boss's Bride *Melanie Milburne*	978 0 263 19983 3
A Wife Worth Waiting For *Maggie Kingsley*	978 0 263 19984 0
Desert Prince, Expectant Mother *Olivia Gates*	978 0 263 19985 7

MILLS & BOON®
Pure reading pleasure™

NOVEMBER 2008 HARDBACK TITLES

ROMANCE

The Billionaire's Bride of Vengeance *Miranda Lee*	978 0 263 20382 0
The Santangeli Marriage *Sara Craven*	978 0 263 20383 7
The Spaniard's Virgin Housekeeper *Diana Hamilton*	978 0 263 20384 4
The Greek Tycoon's Reluctant Bride *Kate Hewitt*	978 0 263 20385 1
Innocent Mistress, Royal Wife *Robyn Donald*	978 0 263 20386 8
Taken for Revenge, Bedded for Pleasure *India Grey*	978 0 263 20387 5
The Billionaire Boss's Innocent Bride *Lindsay Armstrong*	978 0 263 20388 2
The Billionaire's Defiant Wife *Amanda Browning*	978 0 263 20389 9
Nanny to the Billionaire's Son *Barbara McMahon*	978 0 263 20390 5
Cinderella and the Sheikh *Natasha Oakley*	978 0 263 20391 2
Promoted: Secretary to Bride! *Jennie Adams*	978 0 263 20392 9
The Black Sheep's Proposal *Patricia Thayer*	978 0 263 20393 6
The Snow-Kissed Bride *Linda Goodnight*	978 0 263 20394 3
The Rancher's Runaway Princess *Donna Alward*	978 0 263 20395 0
The Greek Doctor's New-Year Baby *Kate Hardy*	978 0 263 20396 7
The Wife He's Been Waiting For *Dianne Drake*	978 0 263 20397 4

HISTORICAL

The Captain's Forbidden Miss *Margaret McPhee*	978 0 263 20216 8
The Earl and the Hoyden *Mary Nichols*	978 0 263 20217 5
From Governess to Society Bride *Helen Dickson*	978 0 263 20218 2

MEDICAL™

The Heart Surgeon's Secret Child *Meredith Webber*	978 0 263 19918 5
The Midwife's Little Miracle *Fiona McArthur*	978 0 263 19919 2
The Single Dad's New-Year Bride *Amy Andrews*	978 0 263 19920 8
Posh Doc Claims His Bride *Anne Fraser*	978 0 263 19921 5

MILLS & BOON®
Pure reading pleasure™

NOVEMBER 2008 LARGE PRINT TITLES

ROMANCE

Bought for Revenge, Bedded for Pleasure *Emma Darcy*	978 0 263 20090 4
Forbidden: The Billionaire's Virgin Princess *Lucy Monroe*	978 0 263 20091 1
The Greek Tycoon's Convenient Wife *Sharon Kendrick*	978 0 263 20092 8
The Marciano Love-Child *Melanie Milburne*	978 0 263 20093 5
Parents in Training *Barbara McMahon*	978 0 263 20094 2
Newlyweds of Convenience *Jessica Hart*	978 0 263 20095 9
The Desert Prince's Proposal *Nicola Marsh*	978 0 263 20096 6
Adopted: Outback Baby *Barbara Hannay*	978 0 263 20097 3

HISTORICAL

The Virtuous Courtesan *Mary Brendan*	978 0 263 20172 7
The Homeless Heiress *Anne Herries*	978 0 263 20173 4
Rebel Lady, Convenient Wife *June Francis*	978 0 263 20174 1

MEDICAL™

Nurse Bride, Bayside Wedding *Gill Sanderson*	978 0 263 19986 4
Billionaire Doctor, Ordinary Nurse *Carol Marinelli*	978 0 263 19987 1
The Sheikh Surgeon's Baby *Meredith Webber*	978 0 263 19988 8
The Outback Doctor's Surprise Bride *Amy Andrews*	978 0 263 19989 5
A Wedding at Limestone Coast *Lucy Clark*	978 0 263 19990 1
The Doctor's Meant-To-Be Marriage *Janice Lynn*	978 0 263 19991 8